The Tale of a Scottish Tower

Yolanda McCall

You are the history of tomorrow!

Best wishes,

Yolanda McCall.

To Peter

Acknowledgements

Particular thanks to: Peter McCall, for contributing so many ideas and for living through every step of this journey with me; Helen Harrold, for her enormous involvement with the structure and content of the early drafts; Pamela McIntyre, for her unabated enthusiasm and for igniting my interest in local history with the 'History of our Streets' nights; Scotland's Urban Past, for captivating me further during the St. John's Tower film project; and Peter Harrold, for writing 'Maria and the Ghosts of Barrengarry,' which inspired me to write this story.

Thanks also to the following people and organisations for providing input, advice or support at various points during the creation of this book: Carnegie Library, National Library of Scotland, Dom Reed, Dave Hallett and Michael Smith at 4edge, The Auld Kirk of Ayr, Fr. John McLean, Elaine Brown, Jane Bristow, Robert Nelmes, Bill Grant MP, Bridget Perks, Holly McIntyre, Allison Wright, Judith Hood, Robert McCall and all the Friends of St. John's Tower.

Finally, a special mention must go to Joseph Yates for his fabulous cover illustration.

Yolanda McCall

One week in Ayr, Scotland ...

Time present and time past
Are both perhaps present in time future
And time future contained in time past.

T.S. Eliot

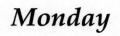

Monday

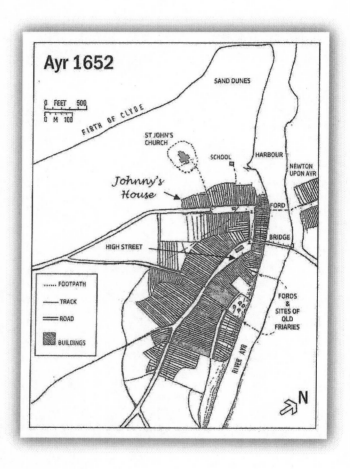

Ayr 1652

FIRTH OF CLYDE

SAND DUNES

ST JOHN'S CHURCH

SCHOOL

HARBOUR

NEWTON UPON AYR

Johnny's House

FORD

BRIDGE

HIGH STREET

FORDS & SITES OF OLD FRIARIES

RIVER AYR

FOOTPATH

TRACK

ROAD

BUILDINGS

N

I

May 1652

Johnny enters the church through the north porch as he does every morning. A rainbow of colours floods through the stained glass window to greet him, and he pauses briefly before walking across the sun-dappled floor. He makes his way into the tower and commences his daily climb up the spiral staircase. All is quiet, except for the increasing rumble of an old man's snores.

Johnny is eleven years old, and he has happily had this routine for the past two years. As usual, his former schoolmaster, Mr Hamilton, is sleeping in his chamber on the third floor of the tower, and Johnny prods his arm saying, "Time to get up, sir," but Mr Hamilton doesn't stir. He tries again, a little firmer this time, but Mr Hamilton continues to snore. Johnny decides to allow his dear old friend to continue his dreams for a minute longer while he trots back down the stairs to the ground floor.

Two ropes dangle though a hole in the ceiling. A huge grin spreads across Johnny's face as he leaps for the ropes and, four floors above, the giant bells swing into action. *Ding-dong, ding-dong, ding-dong, ding-dong*, the bells ring out their call to the town.

Mr Hamilton receives a very rude awakening. He staggers to his feet, snatches his cloak from a hook on the wall, scurries down the stairs and soon appears at the boy's side. "Thank ye, Johnny," he mouths through the loud clanging, "somethin' fir market." and he drops a small coin into Johnny's pocket.

Johnny briefly halts his bell-ringing. "Na, ye shouldna, sir, ye gied me somethin' yesterday," and he feels a touch of regret for the noisy wake-up he gave his kind old teacher.

"Sadly, I fear yer work here may end soon," says Mr Hamilton, and he points through the doorway to where a couple of soldiers have arrived at the back of the church. "The colonel and the major want to speak with ye after the service this morning."

Johnny resumes yanking the ropes and looks across at the soldiers. He is surprised that the colonel and the major want to talk to him, and as he continues ringing the bells, he wonders what it will be about ...

It has been a strange and scary time for Johnny and other people in the town. They have all heard stories of the recent battles in England and Scotland where lots of people were killed. The battles have mostly been about who should rule the kingdoms. The soldiers in Ayr are part of Oliver Cromwell's army, and Cromwell wants the government to be in charge instead of King Charles II; so Cromwell's soldiers are fighting the supporters of the king.

When the soldiers first started arriving last month, Johnny thought there might be a battle in Ayr, but his father explained to him that for most people in Ayr, it doesn't make much difference who rules the country. They will all still have to work hard each day to get enough money to buy food and clothes at the weekly market. And

Johnny's father seems to be right because, so far, all has been calm in their town.

Just a few soldiers rolled up to begin with, on horseback. They stayed at an inn along the High Street and had meetings with the town committee. They went away for a few weeks, but then they returned, and last week a dozen more soldiers arrived. They brought two cannons with them and wagons stacked high with wood and other supplies, and they built stables for their horses beside the church. Then yesterday, another fifty soldiers arrived on foot after marching over a hundred miles from Tantallon Castle. It had taken them five days to reach Ayr and they immediately set up tents behind the church.

Colonel Matthew Alured is the soldier in charge of the troops in Ayr, and he knows it is unsettling for people when an army arrives in town. He wants the people of Ayr to get along well with his soldiers, so last week he spoke at a meeting held in the market place. There were lots of people at the meeting, but Johnny managed to wiggle his way into the hot and stuffy crowd. He couldn't see much, but he could hear everything that was being said.

To begin with, the colonel talked about how pleased he is that Oliver Cromwell sent his regiment to Ayr as he thinks it is a beautiful town. He said he understands that everyone wants to know why they have come, so he would try to explain. He told them that Oliver Cromwell wants to set up five forts in Scotland with soldiers at the ready to fight any supporters of the king.

The colonel then announced, "The forts will be built in Leith, Perth, Inverlochy, Inverness and Ayr. Ayr has been specially chosen to be the main base for Cromwell's army in the south west of Scotland. It is in a great location and has a good harbour for ships to deliver supplies."

He continued, "My soldiers will build a fort with barracks to house over five hundred soldiers. We will build a big wall to create a grand citadel on the high ground above the harbour, and lots more traders will want to visit the town."

He finished by stating, "My troops will need many men to help with all the building work. All the men who are good workers will be paid a fair wage."

Johnny was very happy to hear this because his father is a stone mason and often has to travel far from home for building work. Now Johnny hopes his father will get work building Ayr's Citadel so that he can be home every night and teach him how to build too.

When the colonel made his announcement, Johnny noticed that everyone at the meeting became quite excited. The building of a citadel is good news for the whole town.

So last week most people accepted the army being there. However, since then, the soldiers have started holding meetings in the church and using the church tower to store their armour and weapons, and Johnny knows this is upsetting many folk. But why, he wonders, do the colonel and the major want to talk to him?

Johnny thoughts are disturbed by some tapping on his shoulder. "The minister is ready," Mr Hamilton tells him. Johnny stops ringing the bells. He walks into the main part of the church and the service begins.

II

Present Day

Ding-dong, ding-dong, ding-dong, ding-dong, Martha wakes to the chime of church bells. Her first thought is, have I done all my homework? But she opens her eyes and looks up at the ceiling. It's a very high ceiling, and Martha remembers that she doesn't have school today. It is her summer midterm break, and she is in Scotland, staying with her Aunty Mary and Uncle Peter in their Victorian terraced house in Ayr.

Martha is eleven years old and she is in her first year of secondary school. Her younger sister, Katie, is fast asleep in the bed next to hers. Martha is surprised that Katie can sleep through the noise of the church bells, but she looks to the corner of the room and sees that her little brother, Harry, is also sound asleep with his head dangling over the side of his camp bed. "How can you sleep like that?!" Martha whispers, smirking and shaking her head.

She looks around the room and decides that it isn't as bright and cheerful as her bedroom in Wiltshire. Martha lives in a modern house, and the walls in her room are painted purple. She has stuck pictures of her favourite pop stars and gymnasts all over them and tucked postcards and photos of her friends and family around her mirror.

The children each have their own bedroom at home and Martha thinks that is a good thing. She remembers the squabbles she used to have with her sister when they shared a room a few years ago. But it should be fun to share a room for just a short time, while they are on holiday. There is a pretty tiled fireplace, and she intends to ask Aunty Mary if they can light a fire there one night and toast marshmallows before bedtime.

Martha looks at the clock on the bedside table, only 05:17, but she is wide awake. She gets out of bed and puts on her slippers before walking along the landing to the bathroom. Daylight is sneaking through a gap in the window shutters so, after she has finished using the bathroom, Martha opens them up and glances out the window. It looks like it will be a nice, sunny day, and she notices people entering the old church outside.

Back in the bedroom, Katie and Harry are still both asleep and there is no noise from the rest of the house. Martha opens the curtains slightly so that there is just enough light for her to read. She picks up her history text book: '17th Century Britain.' Martha has one piece of homework to do before she returns to school next week, an essay about life in 17th Century Britain, but she puffs out her cheeks and quietly blows a raspberry. History is her least favourite subject at school. She drops the book to the floor and instead picks up the laptop that the kids all share. This is the ideal time to message her friends before the guaranteed morning fight for computer time will commence.

III

May 1652

As Johnny leaves the church, two soldiers approach him. Johnny knows who they are because they are the smartest looking of all the soldiers and everyone knows who they are. Nevertheless, they politely introduce themselves as Colonel Alured and Major Talbot.

"Now Johnny," says the major, "Mr Hamilton tells us that you are the reliable lad who rings the bells in the tower for the church service each morning."

"Aye, that's right sir," says Johnny, "I always wake at first light, and I've rung the church bells fir the last twa years."

"Well lad, we'd like you to keep doing that, but from now on, the church will only be used for services on Sundays. Any other services will be held in the school house and the school bell will be rung for those."

Johnny is shocked to hear this news. People worship at the church every morning and some go there to pray three times each day. It seems like the soldiers are taking over the church, and he knows that people are already getting upset about that.

"So I'm only to ring the kirk bells on Sundays?" Johnny confirms.

"No. We'd like you to keep ringing the bells every morning, but now it will be to call the workers each day. You should understand that it is a very important job. Many of the men in the town will be helping our soldiers to build the citadel, and it will be your responsibility to wake them up so that they get to work bright and early. Are you happy to do that?"

"Aye, sir, but I dinna think the town folks will be very happy to hear aboot the church services," he dares to say.

"Don't you worry about that lad," Major Talbot assures him, "it will all be discussed at the town meeting tonight."

"We also wanted to speak to you about your father," adds the colonel.

"My faither?"

"Yes. Your father is Mr Adam the stone mason, right?"

"Aye, sir," nods Johnny.

"Is he home today? We'd like to meet him."

"Aye. He was away building hooses in Maybole and Girvan last week, but he's hame the noo."

"We'd like to speak to your father before the town meeting tonight. Would you let him know? We'll be in the tower most of today."

"I'll run and fetch him right noo, sir," and Johnny hurries home straightaway, bursting with the news of everything the colonel and the major told him.

IV

Present Day

As Martha enters the kitchen, she can hear her brother, Harry, asking their Uncle Peter the traditional morning question, "What are you having for breakfast, Uncle Porridge?" Harry is giggling as he waits for the response.

"Porridge of course," replies their uncle, "the breakfast of champions!" Uncle Peter eats porridge for breakfast every morning and that is why, several years ago, Martha and Katie christened him 'Uncle Porridge.'

Uncle Porridge is Scottish, and he loves living on the Ayrshire coast. He is the only Scotsman Martha knows. He has a Scottish accent and occasionally uses funny words, like 'skoosh' or 'ginger' for fizzy drinks, but they can usually understand him, and he always has some Irn Bru in the fridge when they visit. She knows he likes to wear a kilt for special occasions, such as weddings, and he enjoys telling them Scottish stories, such as how a haggis is a little animal that runs around the hillsides with one leg shorter than the other.

He sometimes recites Scottish poetry written by a man called Robert Burns. The poems are in the old Scots language, and Uncle Porridge helps the children to understand what the old words mean; like with the

Scottish song that everyone sings on New Year's Eve called 'Auld Lang Syne.' He told them that the name translates as 'old long since', but really just means 'a long time ago,' and that made good sense.

"Good afternoon!" Uncle Porridge bellows to Martha with a twinkle in his eyes. "What time do you call this? It's nearly lunchtime!"

Martha takes her seat at the breakfast table and fills a bowl with cereal. She smiles, but decides not to rise to her Uncle Peter's bait. It isn't really that late, it is just a traditional greeting that Uncle Porridge fires at the last person to arrive for breakfast.

"Did you sleep well?" asks Aunty Mary.

"Not bad," says Martha, "although I did wake quite early. The church bells woke me up."

Aunty Mary looks a bit puzzled, "Church bells?"

"There aren't any church bells," says Uncle Porridge, "you must have been dreaming."

"Oh, that's a bit odd," Martha giggles, "I thought I saw people going into an old church."

"Maybe you were thinking about the old tower," suggests Aunty Mary.

"Actually, the tower is open today," adds Uncle Porridge, "I was thinking we should go and take a look at it. It's a nice morning so there'll be a good view from the top, and then afterwards we could go to the beach or the shops. How does that sound?"

Everyone nods in agreement. "Shops sounds good," says Martha.

"Beach sounds good," says Harry.

"Will we be allowed to swim in the sea?" asks Katie.

"Oooh," says Aunty Mary, faking a shiver. "I suppose so, if you really want to, but the water will be freezing."

"That won't bother Katie," Martha informs her aunt. She knows that her sister loves swimming and wants to take advantage of every opportunity to get into water, any water, whether it is a river, a lake or especially the sea.

Katie is younger than Martha, yet she nearly always wins if they have a swimming race. Martha doesn't mind. She is pleased that her little sister is one of the best swimmers at the primary school, and anyway, no-one in the family can do cartwheels and back-flips like she can.

"Okay everyone," says Uncle Porridge, "hurry up with breakfast then scoot off and get ready. We'll try to leave in half an hour."

* * * * * * *

It is only a two minute walk to the tower, and Uncle Porridge tells them about its history as they stroll around the wall enclosing its grounds. The children hear that there used to be a big, cross-shaped church attached to the tower. It was called, 'The Church of St. John the Baptist,' and it was built over 800 years ago. It sounds to Martha a lot like the church she thought she saw from the bathroom window this morning. "So what happened to it?" she asks.

"Well," says Uncle Porridge, "the church stopped being used after Oliver Cromwell's army came to Ayr to set up a fort, and eventually it was knocked down."

"My history teacher talked about Oliver Cromwell in our lessons about the 17th century," says Martha, "that's the sixteen hundreds, isn't it?"

"Aye, that's right! Cromwell's soldiers were here in the sixteen fifties, and they built a big wall to protect their fort," continues Uncle Porridge. "The wall went all around the fort and the church and then the area became known as 'The Citadel'."

"Is this the wall here?" asks Harry.

"No," answers Aunty Mary, "that little wall was added in more modern times. The original wall, Cromwell's wall, was much bigger and it enclosed a bigger area. Some parts of the wall are still standing. We can go and see it later."

"That street over there has a sign saying Citadel Place," says Katie.

"Well spotted!" says Aunty Mary, "and the next street over is called Fort Street. Now you know why."

"So what's the difference between a fort and a citadel?" asks Katie.

"There's not really much difference," says her uncle. "A fort is an army base. The term citadel tends to be used for a fort that overlooks or protects a town or a village."

"Citadel actually means little city," adds Aunty Mary, "and this part of Ayr is known as both 'The Fort' and 'The Citadel,' so you can say either and not be wrong!"

They reach the tower and join a queue of people waiting to go inside. While they wait, their aunt tells them about famous people who have visited the area over the centuries, including Kings and Queens, and she says that important meetings were held at the old church.

"And," says Aunty Mary, "there's going to be a play here on Saturday. It will be an outdoor performance and there will be a re-enactment of historic scenes. There will be actors and actresses and musicians, and some of our neighbours are involved too."

"Can we go to that?" asks Katie.

"Of course. You might even be able to join in. One of my friends, Pamela, is organising this year's play. She might still need some children for it. Shall I tell her I have some volunteers?"

"What would we have to do?" asks Katie.

"You would be acting out old times. You'd probably wear old costumes and pretend to be children from hundreds of years ago."

"Can I wear chain mail armour and be a soldier?" asks Harry.

"I'm not sure about that, but I'll ask Pamela. What do you think? Would you like to take part?"

"I'm up for it," says Katie, "it sounds like fun. I like plays."

"Me too," Harry agrees.

"How about you, Martha?"

"Okay, yeah, we might get some photos to post on Instagram. Let's do it. If your friend wants us to that is."

"I'll speak to her and find out!" says Aunty Mary.

* * * * * * *

They enter the tower and on the ground floor there are lots of stone slabs displayed around the walls. "Can you see the carvings on these old tombstones?" says Uncle Porridge. "This one has a sword."

"Why aren't they outside?" asks Harry.

"Well, the slabs were found underground when people came and excavated this area, you know, dug it up looking for proof of the old medieval church; so they probably weren't gravestones like we think of them. Back in the olden days, people generally marked the graves of their loved ones with just a few rocks or a simple wooden cross. These slabs may have come from tombs used for rich or important people buried inside the church."

For Martha, this visit to the tower is beginning to feel like being in Mr Slavin's history class at school. There is a lot of information to take in. She is trying to follow it all, but secretly she hopes they will hurry up and get to the top of the tower, look at the view and then go to the shops. Thankfully, Uncle Porridge soon starts up the spiral staircase.

There is no banister to hold on to and the children carefully follow one behind the other up the narrow steps. Aunty Mary is at the back of their line and she poses a question to them, "Do you know why the staircase in old towers always spirals to the right on the way up?" The children don't say anything. "Show them Peter!" she calls up the stairs.

Uncle Porridge spins around with his right hand held out in front of him. "Imagine I have a sword here in my hand," and he jabs his arm forward. "If I want to defend this tower against people attacking me from below, see how much easier it is for me to use my right arm than it is for you!" He jabs his hand forward again, this time poking Harry in the ribs with his fingers. "And of course most people are right-handed."

Harry is immediately behind Uncle Porridge so, as they enter the first floor room, he holds up his own imaginary sword. "But I can attack you now!" he exclaims, and he lunges towards his uncle.

"Aghh! You got me, Sir Harry," cries Uncle Porridge, as he staggers against the wall. "The tower is now yours!"

The room has a huge fireplace and the children take it in turns to stand inside it, look up the chimney, and see the sky high above. Aunty Mary explains how this room would probably have been used for cooking and eating in the olden days, and she shows them where the toilet, called a dry closet, would have been. Harry is amazed that there is no flush. He thinks it is very funny that everybody's poo and wee would just drop down a chute to be collected at the bottom of the tower. He sits over the hole of the dry closet and makes rude noises while pulling funny faces.

"Did people have toilets in their houses?" asks Katie.

"No, they would have used chamber pots, or a bucket in an outhouse if they had one," answers her uncle.

"Buckets full of poo and wee?!" laughs Harry.

"And a long time ago, people would have tipped the bucket out into the street or the river," adds Aunty Mary, "until they started to realise that all the filth was causing diseases and helping to spread the plague, so then they sent a man with a cart around the town to clear up all the waste and empty people's buckets."

"Oh, that's gross!" declares Martha, screwing up her nose, "I wouldn't want that job."

"Well, it was an important job back in the days before flushing toilets and sewers," says her aunt.

"Okay, I get that, but it's still gross. Can we talk about something else, please?" suggests Martha.

"Yes, let's carry on up," says her uncle and they continue slowly up the twisting steps.

The next two floors each have a room where Uncle Porridge says people might have studied or slept or stored things, and at the top of the tower they find an attic style room with high rafters where the church bells would once have hung. Uncle Porridge tells them that the bells were removed a long time ago, probably when the church was demolished.

Katie counts over one hundred steps in total from the ground floor to the very top of the tower, and finally they find themselves on an outside walkway, just below the roof. They make their way around the parapet and peer over the edge. They can see the tennis courts and the town, and Uncle Porridge points out parts of the old citadel wall. They look at the long row of terraced houses nearby and try to work out which house belongs to their aunt and uncle.

"What's over there?" asks Katie, pointing out to sea.

"That's the Isle of Arran," says Uncle Porridge, "it's about fifteen miles away."

"I'd like to swim over to it one day," says Katie.

"How come the tower is still here?" asks Martha. "Why didn't they pull it down with the rest of the church?"

"I guess they wanted to keep it as a landmark for ships approaching the harbour," says Aunty Mary.

"I think it was used as a lookout tower as well," adds Uncle Porridge. "This old tower will have seen a lot of things in its life. It was here long before our house was built and it would have had a good view of the entire goings on in this town. I bet it could tell a few good tales if only it could talk."

They all take lots of photos before going back down the stairs. Once outside, Uncle Porridge shows them some dimples on one of the outside walls of the tower. He tells them they are pockmarks from where soldiers practised target-shooting with their muskets a long time ago. "We'll go down to the harbour now," he says, "and I can show you the citadel wall up-close."

"And then can we go to the beach?" asks Katie.

It had been bright and sunny earlier in the day, but now it is cloudy. "Let's do shops and cafes today," says Aunty Mary, "it should be sunny all day tomorrow. That will be a better day for the beach. Your grandfather would have called this a GDD."

24

"A Grey Dome Day!" says Martha. "Nonno used to say that, whenever the sky was cloudy and grey all over."

"That's right," says Aunty Mary, smiling. Martha's grandfather, or 'Nonno' as they called him, passed away a couple of years ago and she is really pleased that Martha remembers him.

"A perfect day to go shopping," says Martha.

V

May 1652

Johnny and his mother are sitting by the fire when Johnny's father gets back from seeing the soldiers. "Ye've been away all day," says Johnny's mother, "I hope it's good news."

"There was a lot to talk aboot and I've a lot to tell ye, but first, how are ye, Ena?" he asks his wife.

"No so bad," she replies.

"Maw's still no well," says Johnny, "and I couldna find anythin' in the toon to help her."

"I'm well enough to hear whatever ye talked about wi' the sojers," she says, as Johnny's father pulls a stool over to sit with his wife and son by the fire.

"Do ye remember that I sailed over to the Isle of Arran last year to make repairs to the castle there?" he begins.

"Of course we remember, Paw. You were away fir a whole month."

"Well, the colonel and the major were in Arran last week, and they got talkin' to the grounds man at the castle, and he showed them the work that I did there. He remembered that I live in Ayr, so he recommended that the sojers speak to me aboot their plans fir the citadel."

"Did they show ye the plans, Paw?" asks Johnny.

"Aye, they showed me their maps and sketches. The citadel is going to be huge, aboot twelve acres, and when it's finished it will be a real little city inside, not just a fort. There'll be a bakehouse, a brewhouse and an inn. There'll be housing for the officers, the footmen and for visiting cavalrymen and lots of stables for their horses. They want to build special privy blocks with gutters to take their bucket waste straight into the sea, and they'll have a hospital and their own blacksmith too. They plan to have a great big market place in the middle for all the traders and townsfolk to set up their stalls on market days."

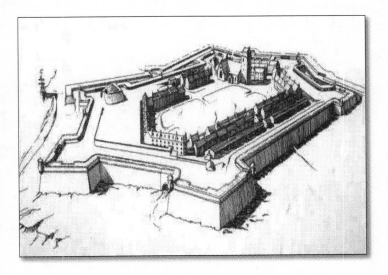

"It sounds braw. Do ye think they can do it?" asks Johnny.

"Well, they're already learning how difficult it is to build on the sand that we have here. I told them that the local stone masons know all aboot that," and Johnny's father continues talking.

He describes how he walked around the land with the officers, behind the church, along the seafront, down to the harbour and back to the church. He made some suggestions for how to make the walls strong, and then the colonel asked him if he would like to be in charge of the building work for the citadel wall.

"Whit did ye say to them, Paw?" asks Johnny.

Johnny's father looks at his wife and son, both waiting eagerly to hear his reply. He manages to catch his wife's eye before saying, "Well I told them I'm not sure I want to take on an important job like that because I'm hoping to teach my son how to hunt."

"But I can already catch rabbits," Johnny points out, "and I need to learn how to build."

"And then they said they will pay me extra money, so I said that if we have extra money I should send my son back to school instead o' teaching him how to carve stone."

"No Paw, I'm nearly twelve, please Paw. I dinna need mair schoolin', I want to be a stone mason."

Johnny's mother starts to giggle, "I think your father's teasing you!" and she bursts out laughing. Johnny's father laughs too and eventually Johnny joins in.

"So whit did ye really say Paw?"

"I said, *yes please* and *thank you*. I start tomorrow."

"It will be so good to have ye home every night with the baby due any day noo," says Johnny's mother.

"I'm pleased about that too," and he pats his wife's big belly.

"Will I be able to help ye with the building work?" asks Johnny.

"Aye, ye'll be working! And ye'll be called my apprentice, but tomorrow is my first day and I'll be busy helping Major Talbot select good workers. Ye start on Wednesday!"

Johnny then asks whether the soldiers said anything about the church services, and Johnny's father confirms the plan that Major Talbot told him this morning. The church will only be used for services on Sundays from now on.

"Naebody will be happy aboot that," says Johnny's mother.

"It'll be announced at the public meeting tonight. I must go there the noo, it's nearly dusk," and Johnny's father leaves for the town.

* * * * * * *

Johnny also goes out. He dashes to the church to set some rabbit snares in the long grass while there is still enough light, and then he runs to the market place in the High Street.

The meeting has already started, and this time the officials are better prepared for a big crowd. They are standing on a raised wooden platform, lit by lanterns, and Johnny can see them quite clearly. He can hear Colonel Alured's loud, deep voice, speaking about how the soldiers need to move into the church, and how the minister will only preach sermons in the church on Sundays and special Holy Days from now on. Johnny feels quite important that he already knew about this.

He is not surprised that a lot of the people become agitated. They start muttering complaints, but the colonel continues, "For the time being, everyone will still be able to visit the kirk to pray whenever they want during the week, and services will be held in the school house on weekdays."

There is a lot of shouting and fist waving, and Johnny thinks there could be a riot until one of the town committee members manages to hush everybody so that the colonel can make a further announcement. "Oliver Cromwell has offered to provide some money for building a new church," he tells them. "It will be a beautiful church, and we will build it near the centre of the town, next to the river, on the site of the old Greyfriars monastery. The new church will be built as soon as the citadel is complete."

The people of Ayr settle down a little on hearing this proposal, and the meeting continues with the colonel announcing that the first selection of workers for all the building work will begin at the harbour in the morning. This reminds everyone that the soldiers are bringing money and work to the town. They are sad to be losing their big old church, but actually they know its roof leaks in several places. The colonel has offered them a fair deal with the promise of a lovely new church, so overall it's not too bad having the army in town.

It is then announced that Mr Adam has been appointed master mason, and this makes Johnny smile from ear to ear. He rushes home to tell his mother about the plan for a new church, feeling very excited about everything. His father now has a very important job. Tomorrow morning he, Johnny, will go and ring the church bells to call the men to work. And on Wednesday, he will become his father's apprentice. Most importantly, he will soon have a little brother or sister. But his excitement turns to worry as he thinks about how sick his mother has been. Surely this time, he hopes, everything will be okay.

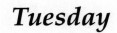

Tuesday

VI

Present Day

Ding-dong, ding-dong, ding-dong, ding-dong, Martha wakes to the chime of church bells. What is making that noise, and how can everyone sleep through that racket again? But Martha feels quite awake, so she hops out of bed, stumbles over her slippers, slips her feet into them and heads to the bathroom. Sunlight is trying to sneak into the room so instead of pulling the light cord, Martha goes straight to the window and opens the shutters, but immediately she shuts them. "Okay, take a deep breath," she mutters, "let's try that again."

Slowly, and with her eyes shut, Martha folds the shutters back into the alcoves on each side of the window. She opens her eyes and looks out the window for a second time. Just as she had thought a few seconds before, there is a church outside. The old tower is still there, but it has a huge church attached to it. The bells stop ringing, and soon after, a boy wearing a flat cap walks out of the church door. This is very odd. She has to check it out.

She starts along the landing, but quickly decides she probably shouldn't go outside on her own, so she knocks on her aunt and uncle's bedroom door.

Aunty Mary leaps out of bed and comes to the door almost immediately. "What is it, Martha? Are you okay?"

"Aunty Mary, there's a church!" Martha whispers. "A really big church. It's right outside. Not just the tower, but a church."

"No Martha, you've been dreaming, it's very early," says her aunt. "Go back to bed, we can check it out later."

Martha isn't going to settle for that. "But I saw it yesterday morning and then it was gone later." She realises how silly that probably sounds, but she is determined to persevere. "Please Aunty Mary, we've got to go outside now. Please!" and Martha takes hold of her aunt's hand, and leads her along the landing and down the stairs.

Once in the hall, Aunty Mary rummages in a drawer full of gloves, quickly finds the right key and opens the big, black outside door of the house. The glare of the sun is very bright, but their eyes soon adjust to the light.

Martha looks outside and her jaw drops. She gapes at what she sees. Only the old tower is standing there. How could she have imagined a church? Had she still been dreaming when she was in the bathroom? This is weird and she feels foolish. She can sense that her cheeks are reddening. "I'm sorry Aunty Mary. I was sure I saw it from the bathroom window."

"Don't worry," says her aunt, "you've just been dreaming. Run back upstairs and get a couple more hours of shut-eye," and Aunty Mary hugs her arm around her niece's shoulders as she ushers her inside.

VII

May 1652

Johnny returns home after ringing the bells in the tower and checking his rabbit snares. He lays a dead rabbit on the dresser and says good morning to his father, then walks through to the back room and out into the yard.

He twists the latch on the doll-sized front door of the little wooden hut that his father helped him to make. The hut rests on an old wooden crate, and three hens file out of their enclosure and toddle down a plank. Johnny reaches his hand inside the hut and feels around in the hay, before taking off his cap and laying it on the ground. He places eggs inside the cap, one at a time, and then carefully carries this package across the yard and into his house. As he enters the front room, his father looks up from spreading some jam on a piece of bread.

"Three the-day," says Johnny, and he smiles as he lays the cap on the table next to his father.

"I see ye caught another rabbit too. How many skins is that ye have noo?"

"That'll be five."

"Well done! You should take them to the tanners in the Sandgate before they dry oot."

"Aye, Paw."

"Your maw's still no well, Johnny, so keep asking aroond for salt and the herbs she needs, and get some onions and carrots from the carts. Buy some bread too."

"Aye, I will, Paw."

"And, gie an egg to Mr McKenzie."

Johnny's dad takes a drink from his cup and stands up. He puts a chunk of bread and a lump of cheese in his pocket and brushes some crumbs off his shirt. He pats his son on the shoulder as he says, "Take care o' yer maw," and he puts on his hat and leaves the house.

Johnny sets a pan of water on the rack over the fire and then goes to his mother's side. She is lying in the box-bed in the corner of the room. "How are ye, Maw?" he asks.

"No so good, son," she says.

"Do ye want some breakfast? There's eggs."

"Na," she shakes her head, "mibbee somethin' later." She takes Johnny's hand and squeezes it. "Dinna fret. I'll be better soon. It's awmost time."

Johnny returns to the fire. The water in the pan is simmering and he gently lowers one of the eggs into it. He slices a piece of bread from the loaf on the table, stabs it with a long fork and holds it over the fire. He stares into the flames and then shuts his eyes. "Please God," he whispers, "keep ma mamma safe." He pauses before adding, "And the wean too. And thank ye fir the eggs this morning."

VIII

Present Day

It's a sunny afternoon and the family are at the beach. Seagulls are squawking, the waves are gently breaking, and Aunty Mary is sitting on a blanket leaning back against the sea wall. She is reading a magazine, but she looks up every now and then to check where everyone is. Uncle Porridge and Harry are playing with a ball by the water's edge. Katie is swimming in the sea.

Martha is paddling. She loves the sensation of the cool water splashing across her feet and ankles, but has no inclination to go for a dip. She has headphones on and is listening to music and quietly singing along. "Ouch!" she cries as the ball strikes her arm.

"Sorry," says Harry.

Martha decides to go and sit with her aunt for a while. They chat about their favourite foods and TV shows, and Aunty Mary asks Martha about her life in Wiltshire. Martha tells her aunt that she now does gymnastics training after school three days each week, and they talk about the amazing gymnasts that they both saw on TV during the Olympics. Martha says that she hopes to be chosen for her school junior team next year.

"How do you like your new school?" asks Aunty Mary.

"It's okay," says Martha, "I've got a good friend called Sarah. She goes to gymnastics with me. The other kids are mostly okay too."

"How about your teachers?"

"They're alright, but they give us lots of homework."

"What subjects do you like?"

"Anything except history."

"Really?"

"Yep, that's the worst. We're doing the 17th century and I don't get it."

"Well, you now know that the 17th century was when Cromwell's Citadel was built here in Ayr. It's when Oliver Cromwell came to power after King Charles the first was killed."

"I suppose so. But it's all pretty confusing and kind of creepy too, learning about dead people."

Aunty Mary tries to think of a way to make history more appealing to Martha. "Do you ever look at the news?" she asks.

"Sometimes, if there's something interesting going on," answers Martha.

"Well history is a bit like reading the news, except instead of it being about what happened yesterday, it's about what happened a long time ago. You're finding out what life was like for people in the past, and some of it is very interesting."

"But there's so much to read to find the interesting bits," grumbles Martha.

"There can be a lot to read," agrees Aunty Mary, "but think of it this way. You use social media, right?"

"Yeah."

"Because?"

"Because I want to find out what my friends are getting up to and tell them my news."

"Well some day in the future, long after you're dead, other kids will probably have to look back at all that stuff you and your friends posted on Instagram and try to work out what life was like in the 21st century."

"Really?"

"Almost certainly. You'll be their history lesson and just think how much there'll be for them to read!"

"That is interesting." Just then Martha's phone beeps. "It's a message from my friend Sarah."

> Going camping tonight
> back Saturday 🐱X

Martha texts back:

> At beach with aunt
> btw you know we're
> the history of
> tomorrow 🔥X

Wednesday

IX

Present Day

Ding-dong, ding-dong, ding-dong, ding-dong, Martha wakes to the chime of church bells. I'm going to ignore it, she thinks. She rolls onto her side, grabs the pillow and pulls it over her head. She shuts her eyes tight. I'm having a dream, just like yesterday. It sounds like a church bell, but it's not a church bell. Ignore it! Dream a different dream!

The dinging noise stops, but Martha can't stop thinking about it. She feels compelled to go and look out the bathroom window. She has to satisfy herself that she isn't going mad; that this isn't some weird recurring dream she is going to have every morning while she is in Scotland, or possibly forever. How crazy would that be? "This has got to stop," she murmurs.

She gets out of bed, looks for her slippers, retrieves them from under Katie's bed and walks to the bathroom. The window shutters are closed and before opening them she pauses at the wash-hand basin. She runs the cold tap and takes a handful of icy water and splashes it over her face. The light is off, so she can't see herself properly in the mirror, but she checks her dim reflection as she pats her face dry with a towel. Her hair is rather messy, but she is sure she looks awake. She can never remember looking at herself in the mirror in a dream! But just to be sure she pinches her cheeks. Ouch! Yes! That is sore, so she decides she must be awake. She will open the shutters, look at the tower, then go back to the bedroom and sleep, or read or play on the lap-top ... and ... as she is telling herself this, she pulls on the little knobs that collapse the shutters back into their day-time homes.

The church is there. She can see it clearly. There is a big old church attached to the tower, and in its grounds she can see a boy darting around, looking for something in the long grass.

Her first thought is to shout out loud and wake the whole household. She could yell, "Help! Come to the bathroom!" She could stand right there by the window and not move. Then she could just keep staring out at the church until Uncle Porridge or Aunty Mary or Katie or Harry or anyone or everyone comes to join her. Then she would be able to point out the window and say, "Look! Look everybody! There's the old church. It's here every morning. You just have to get up early when the bells chime and then you can see it."

But Martha doesn't call out. She keeps staring out the window. Her gaze moves from the church to the boy, to the church and back to the boy, and she thinks about things for a minute.

She tried to show this to Aunty Mary yesterday, but her aunt couldn't see it. In fact the church disappeared. It is possible that Katie or Harry might be able to see the church, but maybe it would disappear again and she really doesn't want them laughing at her.

There must be some reason why she is seeing it. Maybe there is something that she is supposed to do. She doesn't know what that something is, but she feels certain she will keep waking up to the chime of the church bells until she does some investigation and finds out what that something is.

There is an old woollen dressing gown that Aunty Mary said she can borrow hanging on the back of the bathroom door. Martha takes it down from its hook and puts it on over her nightdress. As she heads down the stairs she seems to glide, she barely feels the carpet beneath her feet. She moves towards the hall table to look for the key in its drawer, but before she reaches it, she feels a gush of air as the front door swings open. She takes two paces into the porch and then steps outside.

X

May 1652

Johnny is just checking the last of his rabbit snares when he sees a girl approaching. She looks about the same age as him. "Hello," he says.

"Have you lost something?" Martha asks him.

"Na, I'm lookin' fir rabbits, in ma snares."

"Have you caught any?" Martha hopes that he hasn't. Her sister, Katie, has a pet rabbit at home and she expects this boy isn't trying to catch rabbits for pets.

"Na, not today." he replies.

He had been crouched down and now he drops back to sit there in the long grass, deciding he has time for a little chat. He doesn't recognise this girl and that's unusual. Ayr is a small town with only about two thousand people, so he thinks he knows all the children his age. "Whit's yer name?" he asks her.

"I'm Martha," she says as she sits down on the grass not far from the boy. She is thinking that this whole encounter is very strange. But somehow here she is by the church, and the boy seems to be harmless enough. He has a cheeky grin as he says, "I'm John. Folks call me Johnny," and then he keeps on talking.

He tells her that his mother called him John because she wanted a name that couldn't be shortened. Johnny's mother had been christened Helena, but her family called her Lena and by the time she grew to be a young woman, it was shortened again, to Ena. So his mother thought that John was a good straightforward name. Her son would be named after the patron saint of Ayr and be known as John all his life. Yet instead of his name being shortened, he soon became known as Johnny.

Johnny barely stops to take a breath. Martha decides he is quite a chatterbox, or maybe just nervous. It is probably a good thing that he talks a lot because Martha doesn't recognise all the words that Johnny uses, but he often says something and then says it again slightly differently, so Martha can generally understand him.

"Ye dinna bide here do ye, Martha, where do ye live? Where's yer hame?"

"I'm from England," she answers, "but I'm staying at my Aunty Mary's house."

Johnny chatters on telling Martha about his job of ringing the bells in the tower, and how he is going to be his father's apprentice as a stone mason, and meanwhile Martha tries to think of something to say. Eventually she asks, "What do you do with the rabbits, when you do catch some?"

"Well sometimes I need to bop them on the heed."

"Oh," says Martha.

"If I catch mair than wan, I'll trade them, or I can sell them at market."

"When's the market?"

"On Saturday, every Saturday."

"But sometimes you eat them, the rabbits?"

"Aye, of course."

"I've never eaten rabbit," Martha tells Johnny. He is astonished to hear that, and they chat for a while about what food they like to eat. Johnny tells Martha that now his father has the job of master mason, his family will be able to buy meat or fish to eat most days. He tells her he likes venison and halibut best, and Martha says she's never tried either of them. She says she likes pasta and pizza, but Johnny has never even heard of them.

Johnny doesn't know this girl, but she seems kind, even if some of her words are a bit unusual, and something about her manner makes him feel she might be able to help him. "Ma mither isnae well," he decides to tell her.

"Your mother's sick?"

"Aye. And its awmost time for the wean to be born."

"The wean?" Martha questions.

"Aye, a wean, a baby."

"Oh, your mother's having a baby. Does she need some medicine?"

"She was sick aw night. She needs salt and a good herbal brew."

"Salt?"

"Aye. But the salt pan hooses were destroyed in the storm last month, and the weather was so bad that nae salt traders have come to the market fir three weeks. There is nae spare salt in the toon and nae herbs. Ma maw's herb garden was ruined by the storm."

Martha doesn't know what 'pan hooses' might be, but she is surprised that it could be a big problem to find salt or herbs. Johnny talks some more. He tells Martha that his mother grows herbs and buys spices at the market. She can make special tea to help heal people when they are sick. "She's a folk healer, but now she's sick and naebody can help her."

Then Johnny points his finger towards a woman who has been lingering in the church grounds and is leaning against a nearby tree. "That Maggie Osborne there called ma mither a witch because she heals people. If onyone's a witch it's Maggie Osborne," and Johnny continues, telling Martha that some people say Maggie Osborne has been trying to do evil magic. They think she is responsible for the terrible storms they had recently, and some say she killed a whole family by engulfing their house in snow. "And she's always crabbit," he concludes.

"Crabbit?" asks Martha.

"Bad tempered," says Johnny. "Aye. Nae a good woman."

"Do you really think she's a witch?"

"I dinna ken ..."

"Ken?" interrupts Martha.

"I dinna *know*," continues Johnny, "but if she is, they'll lock her in the tolbooth till she's dead. That's whit they did to Janet Smyllie."

They sit chatting for a while longer until they both notice a tall, bearded man leading a horse and cart towards the church. Martha watches the man jerk the horse to a stop and then remove a shovel from the saddlebag on the horse's back. The man stoops over close to the tower walls and scoops something sloppy into the back of his cart.

"Mr McKenzie is doing his rounds," says Johnny standing up, "I must go and fetch oor bucket."

Martha guesses what might be in the bucket and she determines to keep well clear of it and the smelly cart. "Where will you be after that?" she asks Johnny.

"At the harbour, helping ma faither to build the waw."

"The *waw*?" Martha shrugs her shoulders, she doesn't understand that word.

"The big new wall," he tries to explain, "fir the sojers, fir the citadel."

Martha decides she will go back to the house and see if she can find some medicine to help Johnny's sick mum. She stands up. "I'll go home now," she says, "but maybe I'll see you later," and she turns to leave.

Johnny is already walking away. He turns his head and calls over his shoulder, "Farewell Martha," but she doesn't respond. All the time she was sitting there talking to Johnny, Martha assumed she could get up at any point and go back to the house, but she was wrong. Martha is looking behind her now and she sees that her aunt and uncle's house has gone. It definitely isn't where she thinks it should be. In fact, the whole terrace has vanished and everything looks different.

She looks back towards the church. Two men wearing soldier uniforms are leading horses into stables behind the tower, and beyond the stables she sees rows of tents. It reminds her of a photo that her friend Sarah took of her Girl Guide camp last year. Martha wishes Sarah was with her now. "What's going on?" Martha softly voices.

She starts to run, erratically, towards the beach and then towards the harbour. The house must be somewhere, she must have lost her bearings, but this is beginning to feel like a very bad dream. The whole area is just a piece of wasteland with sand dunes dropping gradually down towards the sea, and three soldiers are working there. One is holding a measuring tape, the second is knocking a post into the ground with a mallet, the third is taking notes and Martha hears him say, "We'll definitely fit two rows of barracks and a stable block inside the wall." He then looks up, sees Martha and asks, "Can I help you, Miss?"

Martha doesn't answer. Her mouth gapes open as she turns and staggers away. How is she going to find the house? Where has it gone? She notices that Maggie Osborne, the woman who Johnny says might be a witch, is coming towards her. "What ... what year is this?" Martha questions Maggie.

"That's a strange thing to ask, lass. It's the year of oor Lord sixteen fifty-two. I'd have thought a big lassie like ye would ken that."

Martha sways in shock. Her mind is reeling. What should she do? Where should she go? She looks around hoping to see where Johnny is, but he is already out of sight. That sour-faced lady is coming up very close, and Martha doesn't like the look of her.

"Whit are ye up to lass?" Maggie asks.

"Nothing," says Martha, "nothing at all."

She jogs back towards the area where she had been sitting with Johnny, but before she reaches it she stumbles on a craggy area of small rocks. She misses her footing and flies up into the air ...

XI

Present Day

Aunty Mary is in the kitchen unpacking the dishwasher when she hears a loud clatter at the front of the house. She dashes to the hall and sees Martha lying in a heap at the bottom of the stairs. Uncle Porridge has just beaten her to the scene and is speaking to his niece and helping her to her feet.

"Martha! What happened? Come on, let me help you up."

"The church was back again. Did you see it?" mutters Martha.

"Oh Martha!" says Aunty Mary. "Are you okay? Did you have another dream? Did you slip on the stairs?"

"I think you've banged your head, take your time," says Uncle Porridge. "Here, sit on the bottom step. Do you remember what happened?"

Martha is a little dazed and Uncle Porridge and Aunty Mary both seem to be talking at the same time. "Do you think you might have been sleep-walking?" asks her uncle.

"We may need to get you checked over at the hospital instead of going to Glasgow today," says her aunt. The plan has been for all the family to spend the day in the city.

Eventually they allow Martha to speak, and in between more questions she tells them that she thinks she is okay. Yes, she has knocked her head, but no, she's sure she doesn't need to go to hospital. She doesn't think she was sleep-walking, although yes, maybe she did have another weird dream. Martha tells them she does feel quite tired and maybe it would be nice to have a quiet day at home instead of rushing for the train, "But I know Harry is really looking forward to the train journey," she finishes up.

"You are a bit peely-wally," says Uncle Porridge.

"I'm a bit what?!" asks Martha.

"Just a bit pale, love," says her aunt.

"I'd be very happy to stay home and keep working on the car today," offers Uncle Porridge. "Martha can have a relaxing day and I'll make sure she's okay."

And so it is settled. Aunty Mary, Katie and Harry catch the train to Glasgow. Martha and Uncle Porridge stay at home.

* * * * * * *

Martha is sitting at the kitchen table colouring. The radio is on and every now and then one of her favourite songs comes on and Martha sings along. She feels a bit tired, but otherwise she is absolutely fine. She thinks about her early morning experience. She certainly bumped her head, she has a small lump on her forehead to prove it, but did she dream the rest? She continues with her colouring and Uncle Porridge pops in and out of the kitchen occasionally, usually with dirty oil on his hands.

They have lunch together and afterwards Martha goes out to the garage with her uncle and they chat about the old car he is working on. Uncle Porridge tells Martha that his cousin used to own the car and he bought it from him.

"Do you have lots of cousins?" Martha asks.

"No, Robert's the only one. I don't have many relatives at all," he replies.

They talk some more, but soon Martha feels tired, so she goes to the bedroom for a lie down. She falls asleep quite quickly, and when she wakes up she lies there for a while thinking about the dream she just had. It was a silly dream with Harry and Katie and they were ... they were ... what were they doing? Martha tries to remember, but she has forgotten already. It was just a dream, but it makes her realise that what happened to her this morning definitely wasn't a dream.

She can vividly recall every part of the incredible episode: leaving the house, sitting on the grass and talking to the boy wearing a flat cap. They chatted about rabbits and food and his sick mother. His name was Johnny, and then there was a strange woman who was called Maggie something, "Maggie Osborne," Martha says the name out loud and sits up in bed. You can never remember names in dreams, but Martha can remember these names, and she can remember the smell. The air smelled different from the moment she went outside; it was musty with a strong whiff of fish and a nasty stench when the man with the horse and cart arrived. And there were sounds too: the neighing of the horses when they were led into the stable, and the clonk of the mallet hitting the post when the soldier spoke to her.

"I actually travelled back in time to sixteen fifty-two!" Martha declares to the empty bedroom. It is mind-blowing, but she is certain it is true. She has had an actual encounter with the past. The more she thinks about it, the faster her heart beats as she grasps the enormity of what has happened to her. She tries to stay calm, to study the facts, but she is finding it impossible. She grabs her phone and tries to call her friend Sarah, but it goes straight to voice mail so she sends a text:

> Crazy morning
> travelled back to 1652
> call me pls X

Martha keeps her phone in her hand, willing it to ring or at least buzz with the arrival of a text. Nothing happens. She recalls Sarah's message yesterday saying that she was going camping; she probably doesn't have a phone signal. Martha sighs. She's going to have to work this out for herself.

She attempts to logically think through all the events of the last few days. On Monday morning she saw the old church, but it wasn't there later when Uncle Porridge took them to visit the tower. On Tuesday morning she saw it again, but it wasn't there when she went outside with Aunty Mary. This morning she successfully went outside to the time of the old church and she was on her own. That means if she is to travel to 1652 again, definitely no adults can be included, and it is likely to happen after she has just woken up and - suddenly it dawns on Martha that she has just been asleep and now she is awake - she immediately runs to the bathroom.

She looks out the window, but she sees no church, no Johnny, no soldiers, no 17th century life; just cars in the street and the old tower standing tall and proud with its flag hanging limply. She sits on the window seat and ponders some more. Why does the church only appear in the mornings? Does it have something to do with Johnny? Or something to do with the chiming of the bells?

She feels a bit despondent. A remarkable thing happened to her and she doesn't know if it will ever happen again. She wasted her chance on Monday and again on Tuesday, and then today she panicked and wanted to return to the present day when perhaps she could have stayed longer and witnessed something really important. If she'd gone with Johnny she might have seen the citadel wall being built, but she blew it. How could she have messed up something so special? She will be embarrassed to tell Sarah the whole story.

Now Martha feels really down. She touches the sore bump on her forehead from her fall this morning. If only she could have stayed calm instead of running and tripping, but it was such a shock when she discovered that her home was missing, and she didn't want to be near that witchy woman either.

She stares at the dressing gown hanging on the back of the door with its big patch pockets and she comes up with a plan. It would be really nice to spend more time with Johnny and learn about his life in 1652, but she has to accept that she has no control over it. Hopefully she will get another chance to go back in time. If she does, she should be prepared.

* * * * * * *

Martha goes downstairs and looks for her Uncle Peter. Not surprisingly, she finds him in the garage.

"Did you manage to sleep?" he asks.

"I did, thank you and I feel much better and I've been thinking, it's Katie's half-birthday today."

"Oh. So she's ... nine and a half?" he guesses.

"Yes," says Martha.

"And you would normally celebrate that?"

Martha hesitates. "Let's say yes," she replies. "I was thinking about baking a cake for her. Would that be okay? Can I look in the cupboards to see if the ingredients I need are there, or do you think I should text Aunty Mary first?"

"No need, I know she bought in lots of extra stuff in case you three wanted to do some cooking. Just please don't use any metal knives or spoons on her non-stick pans, that drives her crazy."

"Don't worry, my mum has the same rule."

"If it's Katie's half birthday, she really only needs half a cake, doesn't she? So how about we eat half, and you could ice the other half to give to her?!"

"I can't believe you suggested that! Well, maybe ... or maybe I'll make some cookies as well. I learned a new recipe in H.E. last week."

"H.E?"

"Home economics."

"Ah, right. Well, just give me a shout when you want to use the cooker. Remember you banged your head this morning, I don't want you burning yourself."

Martha returns to the kitchen. Great, she thinks. She has a couple of easy baking recipes in mind, but the real reason she wants to look in the cupboards is to gather stuff for Johnny, or more precisely, for Johnny's sick mother.

She uses a stool to get up to the high cupboard where her aunt keeps cough syrup and other medicines. She finds a variety of bottles and boxes, each holding tablets and capsules, but every item comes with instructions and warnings about taking medicine that the doctor hasn't prescribed for you. She finds a sachet of rehydrating salts: 'Essential Minerals to restore health after sickness or diarrhoea.' It is probably exactly what is needed, but Martha knows this will look very unusual in 1652. Will Johnny's mother want to drink something that looks and tastes so different from what she is used to? Martha remembers Johnny saying, "She needs salt and a good herbal brew."

Martha abandons the medicine cabinet in favour of the big pantry and quickly finds a large tub of rock salt. She doesn't want to take the whole tub, but luckily there is a small glass jar on the draining board. She makes sure the jar is dry, pours salt into it and then screws the lid on tight. What else? she wonders.

She fetches the lap-top and looks up 'natural remedies for sickness,' and discovers that ginger root or camomile can be used for calming an upset stomach. She also finds many other suggestions for healing various ailments using garden herbs.

Martha returns to the pantry and hunts through the shelves ... flour, sugar, sultanas and "Yes!" she exclaims, as she finds a piece of ginger root. Then she takes a pair of scissors from the cutlery drawer and goes into the garden. She finds her aunt's herb patch, but she has no idea what to pick. One plant smells of lemon, another mint, and perhaps another is rosemary. There are others herbs whose names she can't even begin to guess, but she snips lots of leaves from the fragrant plants and takes them all into the kitchen.

Martha gathers everything together on a tray – the herbs, the ginger root and the jar of salt – and takes it upstairs to the bathroom. Here she loads all the items into the pockets of the dressing gown. Then she returns to the kitchen to do some baking.

* * * * * * *

The cakes and cookies are cooling, well most of the cookies because Uncle Porridge has already stolen two, and Martha is doing some colouring at the kitchen table when her brother and sister burst in after their day visiting Glasgow.

"You missed a brilliant film at the IMAX," Katie tells her. "I felt like I was underwater, swimming with sharks and jellyfish!"

"What did you like, Harry?" Martha asks.

"Well," he pauses, struggling to remember.

"Did you go to the Science Centre?" she prompts him.

"Yes, we did ..." he pauses again.

"And? Was it good?"

He ponders the question. "Yes, but I think the best bit was catching the train. There are so many trains in Glasgow, Martha, I've never seen so many trains and we had yummy hot chocolate in the station."

"So, Aunty Mary took you all over Glasgow and the bits you remember best are the train and the hot chocolate?!" Martha giggles.

"It was very good hot chocolate," confirms Katie.

"How are you feeling, Martha?" asks Aunty Mary as she enters the kitchen.

"Great, thank you. I've had a nice relaxing day and," she points to the cake on the counter, "now we can celebrate Katie's Half-Birthday!"

"Yay!" shouts Katie. "Thank you!" and she gives her sister a big hug.

Thursday

XII

Present Day

Ding-dong, ding-dong, ding-dong, ding-dong, Martha wakes to the chime of church bells. She jumps out of bed, squeezes into the wrong slippers, kicks them off, finds her own and then hurries to the bathroom. She opens the shutters. Wow! The church is back. She plonks herself down on the window seat and nervously bites her bottom lip as her heartbeat rapidly increases. Ooh, this is really happening. Again.

She grabs the dressing gown and checks the pockets as she puts it on over her nightdress. The left pocket holds the jar of salt and the piece of ginger root. The right pocket is stuffed full with the herbs she collected in the garden yesterday. Some of the herbs have wilted a little, but she is quite sure they will be fine. Even dried herbs are better than no herbs.

She takes another look out the window and spots Johnny. He is walking in the direction of the harbour. She goes downstairs and just as she reaches the big, black front door, before she even touches the handle or looks for the key, it swings open. She pauses in the doorway for a moment, looking at the church and the tower. Martha is usually pretty sensible and she feels somewhat uneasy about what might lie ahead. She wants to visit 1652, she wants to give Johnny the herbs and the salt for his mother, and she would like to talk to him some more, but she is not sure how she will return. And what if Maggie Osborne is hanging around? She would rather not meet her again.

Martha pokes her head out the door and looks around. Thankfully there is no sign of Maggie, but Johnny is now out of sight. If she is going to go, she knows it has to be now, while she still has a good chance of catching up with him and before the church decides to disappear.

She stands in the porch and holds the doorframe, swinging her right leg backwards and forwards. Present day or yesteryear? None of this is logical yet it seems that even her aunt and uncle's house is encouraging her to leave. Why else would the front door have opened by itself? She takes a deep breath, lets go of the doorframe and steps outside.

XIII

May 1652

Martha immediately looks behind her. She sees that the long row of terraced houses, where her aunt and uncle live, has again ceased to exist. Her heart is still beating fast, but she mutters, "Okay." She takes another deep breath, carefully notes how far she is from the tower and then kicks a few stones together to make a small mound. Only when she is sure that she has her position marked well enough does she set off in the same direction that she saw Johnny walking a few minutes earlier.

An increasing babble of voices and screeching seagulls accompanies Martha to the harbour. When she gets there, she finds it is a hive of activity. One busy boat has already moored and soldiers are unloading large chunks of rock from it. A second boat arrives and men tip fish and shellfish from big nets into baskets and pass them to women standing on the shore. There are several soldiers talking in a huddle, and another soldier is issuing instructions to a group of men standing by a pile of rocks where the citadel wall is being built.

She spots Johnny by the wall. A man is talking to him and showing him how to scrape a chisel along a stone block in a particular way.

"Johnny?" she calls, "hello."

"Hello!" he calls back, "this is ma faither. He's teachin' me how best to sharpen the tools."

"Hello," says Martha, and Johnny's father smiles and nods his head towards her while tipping his cap.

Johnny exchanges a few words with his father then walks towards Martha and guides her to a quieter place towards the mouth of the river, away from the hustle and bustle of the harbour.

"I've brought you some things, for your mother," she says, and she takes a handful of herbs from her pocket to show him. Then she rummages in the other pocket and lifts out the ginger root and hands it to Johnny. Finally she offers him the jar of salt.

He is uneasy at first. "Where did ye find aw this?"

"In my Aunty Mary's house."

"I cannae take it frae ye."

"Take it, please. Seriously."

He looks at her eager face and realises she means it. "I will take it, but happily, nae seriously. This is braw. Are ye sure yer aunty can spare it aw?" Johnny is studying the little glass jar of salt intensely and tries to prise the lid off. Martha shows him how to twist the lid to open it.

"That's fabulous! But ye should keep that, it'll cost a lot at market. Ye shoudna take it frae yer aunt."

"Whatever," says Martha, thinking that the jar will probably just be chucked in the recycling bin unless her aunt plans to make some jam soon. "The herbs were in my aunty's garden. She has masses of them ... in a sheltered spot. The rest of it was in her kitchen cupboard."

"She'll skelp ye when she finds oot whit ye took."

"No, she won't mind. Where I come from we have lots of stuff like this. I can easily get her more from the Co-Op ... I mean from the market."

"Where do ye come frae?"

"My home is in Wiltshire."

"And that's in England?"

"Yep."

All of the soldiers in the town come from England, but Martha is the first girl from England that Johnny has met. She dresses a bit differently from the local girls, and she definitely talks differently, but he can understand most of what she says. "Ma mither is gaun to be so happy when she sees aw this. I'll gie ye the next rabbit I catch. Or twa rabbits?"

Martha shakes her head. "No, it's a gift. I hope your mother gets better."

Johnny notices that Maggie Osborne is nearby again and he fears she may have seen all the wonderful things that Martha has given him. He decides it's time to move on. "I'll take it to ma maw right noo. Come wi' me?"

It's a question, but Johnny doesn't wait for an answer. He has already taken one step up the steep bank, and he stretches out his hand for Martha to grasp and follow him.

At the top of the rise, Martha notices some children coming out of a small building overlooking the harbour. "Is that a school?" she asks.

"Aye, that's oor school. We've had a school in Ayr for hundreds of years. It started in St. John's Kirk as a church school, but it moved into that hoose some time ago."

They cross a wide open area and Martha sees some soldiers come out of the church and line up in three rows. A whistle is blown and a flag is hoisted at the top of the tower; it is black, but has a red cross on a white square in the corner of it. The whistle sounds again and the three rows start marching around, following orders bellowed by a short, fat soldier.

"All these soldiers," says Martha, "are they part of Oliver Cromwell's army?"

"Aye, that's right. The first arrived a few weeks ago and then dozens mair on Sunday."

"So who is Oliver Cromwell, Johnny? And what are the battles all about?"

"Oliver Cromwell is noo the chief commander of the government's army. Cromwell doesnae think the king should rule the country. He wants the government to rule the country. So, most of the battles have been between Cromwell's army and the supporters of the king."

"And that's King Charles the uh ... second?"

"Aye. King Charles the first was killed three years ago and his son, King Charles the second, has gone into hiding. Ye must ken that?"

"Yes, I did hear that," and Martha thinks back to her school history class, "but it's good to have it all explained again. Thanks Johnny."

"Look oot Martha!" Johnny warns as Martha narrowly misses stepping in a pile of horse manure.

* * * * * * *

Quite soon they reach Johnny's house. It is the first in a row of six stone cottages with thatched roofs. Martha pauses at the door. "This is where you live?"

"Aye. My paw built these hooses. We used to live in a wooden hoose by the river, but this is much better. Come in."

There is no lock on the door. Johnny pushes it open and Martha follows him inside. A rain cloud is passing over so, even though there is a window, it is a little dark inside and Martha automatically looks for a light switch. There isn't one, but her eyes soon adjust and she looks around to take in her surroundings.

There is a wooden dresser with cups and plates neatly arranged on its shelves, and a wooden dining table with a bench and two stools around it. Martha can see no electric lights anywhere in the room, but there is a candle in a metal holder sat in the middle of the table, and she spots a couple of oil lamps and candlesticks on a shelf above a fireplace.

It is a large open fireplace with the remains of a fire smouldering in the hearth. Two black metal pots and a black kettle rest beside it. On one side of the fireplace there is a basket filled with what Martha thinks might be coal. On the other side of the fireplace there is a second basket, full of chopped up wood and twigs, and a wooden armchair sits in front of it.

There is an alcove in the corner of the room with a curtain draped part of the way across and Martha realises that it is a bed and that there is a woman in the bed, who appears to have been sleeping but is now pulling herself up to a sitting position. The lady in the bed looks pale and sickly and a large tummy bump is visible under the covers.

"This is ma mither," says Johnny, "Mrs Adam," and he introduces Martha, and shows his mother the ginger and the herbs that Martha has given them. Martha is about to say that her Uncle Peter's surname is also Adam, but she can see that Johnny's mum isn't at all well. She doesn't think it's a good time to start that sort of conversation. Perhaps she'll tell Johnny later.

Mrs Adam beckons Johnny closer and he holds a handful of herbs to her face so that she can see and smell how fresh everything is. She smiles weakly and looking at Martha she whispers, "Thank ye," and she points towards the fireplace.

Martha

Johnny lifts the heavy black kettle and loops its handle onto a hook that hangs from a chain above the open fire. He then adds some twigs and coal to the smouldering ash and pokes at the fire with an iron rod until flames burn brightly. His mother tells him to chop a tiny piece of the ginger, and then she picks a selection of leaves from a bundle in Johnny's hands. Johnny puts these in a cup with the ginger he has chopped. When the water comes to the boil he pours it into the cup, adds a teaspoon of honey from a small clay pot and leaves the cup on the table for a few minutes.

While the infusion is brewing, Johnny empties the jar of salt into an empty clay pot. He gives the glass jar to Martha and offers the pot of salt to his mother. His mother gasps in shock and delight. She licks a finger, dips it into the pot of salt and then pops it in her mouth. The idea of eating raw salt would normally make Martha cringe, but today she is fascinated that such a simple gift could be so appreciated. Johnny hands his mother the cup of herbal brew, and Martha watches closely as Mrs Adam sprinkles a pinch of salt in it before starting to sip.

Martha and Johnny leave the room and walk through to a second room. Just as in the first room, there is no wallpaper and there are no pictures on the walls. Martha sees a shelf with a couple of books and an oil lamp on it and there is a small wardrobe and a chest of drawers with a jug and a basin sat on the top. There are two wooden beds, each with a frame supporting a canopy and curtains. They are a bit like the four-poster bed that Martha remembers a princess having in a picture storybook she once read, except these beds are much plainer looking.

"Is this where you sleep Johnny?"

"Na, I sleep where ma Mamma is, but she needs to be near the fire just noo as she's no well."

They move through the room and sit on the back doorstep, looking out at a yard shared with the other cottages in the lane. Beyond the yard there are fields with sheep and cattle grazing.

Martha spots a goat, tied by a long rope to the back door of the next cottage. It is straining its leash, trying to reach a nearby plot containing a few ragged, storm-battered plants. She sees some chickens pecking at the ground in a fenced off area with a small wooden hut, and directly behind Johnny's house there is a lean-to shack with some buckets and three large barrels outside it. Martha hasn't seen a sink anywhere and she wonders if the barrels are used to collect rainwater.

The sun comes out and they feel its warmth on their faces. Johnny rolls up his grubby sleeves and Martha notices that his arms are just as dirty underneath. "Look at the colour of you! You're all dirty. When did you last have a bath?" she jokingly asks him.

"I have a bath every year on ma birthday whether I need it or no! I'm no durtie, ye're just peely-wally. Does the sun no shine where ye come frae?"

"Of course the sun shines, but I wear factor 30 and I take a shower every day."

Johnny is a bit puzzled. Did Martha say there is a rain shower every day? It often rains in Ayr, but not every day and there is usually some place to take shelter when it does rain.

"Do ye work inside or ootwith?" he asks.

"I don't work!" she laughs, "I go to school. Don't you go to school?"

"I went to school fir twa-three years and I was taught music, and reading and writing in Latin and English, and I ken ma numbers too."

"But you don't go anymore?"

"Na. I'm nearly twelve. It's mair important that I help ma mither and faither and learn how to build."

"I'm eleven and I have to go to school for another five years, maybe longer," says Martha, "and it's hard. Not so much the being at school, but all the homework. And they say there'll be even more next year. I'm a bit worried about it actually."

"I'm frettin' aboot the wean," says Johnny.

"You're fretting? You're worried about the baby that your mother's having? I'm sure there's nothing to fret about," says Martha.

But Johnny has more to share with Martha. He tells her that last year his mother had a baby. Johnny clearly remembers everything about that day. His father was away, it was tea time and his mother was spooning some soup into his bowl when she gasped and dropped the ladle. She sent him to fetch a neighbour, Mrs Craig, and then he waited outside for hours and hours. When at last he was allowed to go in, his mother was crying. She was holding the baby and it was a wee lass, a tiny beautiful wean, but she wasn't breathing, she didn't move at all. She was pale and still and her lips were blue.

"Mrs Craig called her Stillborn. We called her Grace," he finishes.

"Oh, I'm so sorry," says Martha, and she pictures her sister, Katie, lying motionless with blue lips and her face totally pale without her normal sprinkle of sun freckles. It's a horrible thought. They are both silent for a while before Martha says, "I've got a little sister, called Katie. She's a bit annoying at times, but I couldn't bear to lose her. I've got a funny wee brother too, called Harry."

"I had twa wee brothers, but I dinna remember them much," says Johnny. And he tells her that his two younger brothers died during the plague of 1647. Martha finds this unimaginable.

"That's awful!" she exclaims, "that is so sad. Couldn't the doctor do anything to save them?"

"The doctor who teaches at the school? Or do ye mean the man frae Edinburgh? The physician he called himself. The town folk accused him of sorcery and he didnae bide lang."

"Is there a hospital in Ayr?"

"Aye, in Mill Street, by the auld friaries. They help the very auld and they feed the very poor, but they cannae cure the plague."

Johnny tells Martha that his brothers and his baby sister are all buried near the church. His father had put wooden crosses to mark their graves, but they blew away in the last storm. Johnny then says that he has heard of people carving grave markers out of stone, 'headstones' he thinks they are called. "Do ye ken?" he asks.

"Yes," she answers, "I've seen headstones on graves."

"When I'm a stone mason, I want to make a big headstone fir ma brothers and ma wee sister. Somethin' that will always be there. But fir noo," and he stands up, "I have to go and help ma faither at the waw. If I do a good job, the sojers will gie me work building the new kirk."

"The new kirk. That's a church isn't it? There's going to be a new one?"

"Aye, Oliver Cromwell has said he will gie some money to build a new kirk because the sojers have taken over St. John's."

They say goodbye and Johnny sets off back to the harbour.

* * * * * * *

Martha walks to the church and crosses the grassy area in front of it to reach the rough piece of ground where she tripped and fell yesterday. She checks her position in relation to the tower and quickly finds the mound of stones that she made earlier. She knows that the stones mark a position right outside her aunt and uncle's front door in the

21st century. She is in the right place. She just needs to work out how to get back to her right time.

She has an idea that the spot where she fell yesterday must be some sort of sweet spot. Perhaps there is a hidden gateway that will take her back to her own time. She remembers that the place where she actually fell is probably a little nearer to the sea because when she stumbled she landed in her aunt's hallway. So she walks to and fro a few times, but she can see nothing unusual on the ground. No patch of earth appears in any way special or different from the rest of the area. And despite her walking backwards and forwards and all around the site several times, she is still stuck in 1652.

She wonders if she needs to be flying through the air to open the gateway, so she runs and she leaps. She tries jumping, as high as she can, and she leaps again and turns cartwheels and does a back-flip. It doesn't work, and Martha begins to get concerned. Maybe it was because she was knocked out yesterday? Surely she doesn't have to fling herself at the ground and bang her head again?

Meanwhile, Martha is being watched. Maggie Osborne now approaches her. "Whit are ye up to lass? Aw thae jumps and leaps, are ye making magic and spells?"

"No, of course not. I'm ... I'm practising my gymnastics."

"I saw ye appear oot o' thin air yesterday and then later ye disappeared. Is that whit ye're trying to do noo? And where did ye get thae lovely fresh herbs and the salt that ye gied Mrs Adam's son?"

Martha doesn't want to talk about it. She turns to walk away, pretending she didn't hear what Maggie asked, but the woman pounces after her and grabs her arm. Martha gets spun around and finds Maggie's menacing and screwed up face so close to her own that she can smell the woman's horrible breath and see the gaps in her teeth.

"I think ye're a witch," says Maggie. "If ye tell me whit ye're doing, I willnae need to report ye. It will be oor secret."

"Please leave me alone."

"Or ye could gie me yer fancy goon or thae wee, soft shoes and I'll be on ma way."

Martha steps backwards again, but Maggie is still holding her arm. There is a short struggle and Martha manages to break free. She runs as fast as she can to Johnny's house, opens the door and slams it shut behind her. She turns and sees Johnny's mum sitting bolt upright in the bed, looking somewhat shocked. Martha immediately says sorry. She explains that Maggie Osborne has been bothering her and asks if she can please stay for a while.

"Maggie Osborne is nae friend o' mine, Martha. Ye can bide as lang as ye want." Johnny's mother lies back down and Martha sits in the chair by the fire, thankful that Maggie didn't dare to follow her into Johnny's house.

She looks around the room. It is basic, but Martha thinks she could live in it, for a few days anyway. It would be a challenge trying to live without electricity, like being on some game show. If her friend Sarah was with her it could actually be fun.

Through the window, Martha can see that Maggie is waiting outside. She is sitting on the ground and is scratching herself then examining things in her finger nails. Martha shudders; she hopes she doesn't catch fleas from that unpleasant woman.

She wonders how long it will take for Maggie to get bored and leave and she comes up with a plan. If Maggie hasn't left by the time Johnny gets home, she will sit him down, tell him to stay calm, and then tell him where - or rather when - she comes from. It may be hard to persuade him that she comes from the future, but she will have to try. She will need his help to get back to her own time.

At least she is safe for now. It is cosy in Johnny's house and the chair is quite comfortable. Martha stares at the fire, hoping and praying that Maggie will go away, but before Maggie goes away and before Johnny gets home, Martha drifts off to sleep.

XIV

Present Day

Martha wakes up and takes in her surroundings. She is sitting on a wooden armchair in the corner of the garage where Uncle Porridge is working on his car. The bonnet is open, and he is bent over the engine.

"Uncle Porridge," she begins and then, "sorry!" as her uncle swiftly raises his head and bangs it on the bonnet.

"Ow! Oh! I didn't think anyone was up yet," he rubs his head. "You're up bright and early."

"I feel like I've been up all night."

"What? Didn't you sleep?"

"Well, yes, but I woke up early. Uncle Porridge, where did this chair come from?"

"That tatty old chair you're sitting on?"

"Yes."

"Your Aunty Mary picked that up a few weeks ago from a junk shop in Newmarket Street. She thinks it could be quite old. The varnish is peeling off and it needs to be rubbed down. It needs some TLC."

"TLC?"

"Tender loving care. Then it might be quite charming, it does have a lovely arched back."

Martha walks around the chair studying it carefully. She has no doubt that it is the exact same chair that was in Johnny's home. She can't quite believe her luck. She fell asleep on this old chair in 1652 and woke up sitting on it in her aunt and uncle's garage.

"I think it should be on the Antiques Roadshow," says Martha.

"Well it probably needs to be tidied up first, so if you want to make yourself useful!" Uncle Porridge hands Martha a piece of sandpaper from his toolbox.

"Maybe after breakfast, or maybe later," says Martha, and she puts the sandpaper back where it came from. "Uncle Porridge, you know how the other day you said that the old church by the tower was knocked down hundreds of years ago. Do you know if they built a new church?"

"They sure did. It's now known as the Auld Kirk," and Uncle Porridge smiles, thrilled that his niece is curious about Ayr's history. "Do you want me to take you there? It's not far."

Martha nods, "Yeah, I'd like to see it."

"Okay, go inside and grab some breakfast. I'll be along shortly. We can probably be there and back before your brother and sister get up."

* * * * * * *

Martha and her uncle set off on foot to visit the Auld Kirk. On the way, Martha asks if there is a school nearby, and Uncle Porridge takes her on a slight detour to see an impressive looking school. It is much bigger than the wee schoolhouse that she saw in Johnny's time. Uncle Porridge tells Martha that there's been a school on that site for hundreds of years. She nods, and just manages to stop herself from saying, "Yes, I know, I saw it!"

Next they cut through a courtyard next to an old building with wooden balconies. Martha remembers seeing it when she was at the harbour with Johnny and she asks Uncle Porridge if he knows anything about it. He tells her it's called Loudoun Hall. "It's one of the oldest houses in Ayr," he says, "I think it once belonged to the Sheriff of Ayrshire."

Martha thinks she better bear that in mind for the future ... but, no, she corrects herself ... for the past.

They cross into the High Street and at a bend in the road there is a statue of a man holding a fish. "This place is known as the Fish Cross," her uncle tells her, "it's where the fish were traditionally sold after the boats came into the harbour."

They continue walking and soon turn left along a cobbled close, then pass through a stone gateway to reach the Auld Kirk. The church sits in a pretty grassed area next to the river, and they stroll around and admire its arched windows. Martha spots a cornerstone that has been carved to display the year 1654. She gasps and puts her hand to her mouth as she thinks about Johnny helping to build this beautiful old church.

They leave through the graveyard, behind the church, and Martha takes in the street names as they walk back towards the High Street ... Blackfriars Walk, then Mill Street. She remembers Johnny saying that the hospital was in Mill Street, near the old friaries, but there is no sign of a hospital or a friary now. Then she sees some interesting stone sculptures of plants and bowls high up on a wall.

"Look at this Uncle Porridge" and they both read the sign on the wall: 'This wall stands on the site of the 13th *century monastery of the Black Friars where they grew herbs for medicine.'*

On their way back home, Martha looks out for the row of cottages where Johnny lives in the 17th century, but she can't see any cottages in the town. There are lots of old buildings, but they are all two or three storeys high and she realises that Johnny's wee house must be long gone.

Just before they reach the tower, Uncle Porridge takes Martha along Citadel Lane where they find another commemorative inscription above an arch in the wall: *'Citadel Gate: this was the main gateway to the citadel fort.'*

Martha thinks about the layout of the big church that stands beside the tower in Johnny's time, and she tries to picture it surrounded by a fort with a huge wall to protect it. That would be an incredible thing to see. She hopes she will get a chance to visit Johnny when the citadel is complete.

They resume their walk home and, as they pass the tower grounds, Martha notices one single gravestone. "Do you know anything about that gravestone?" she asks, pointing towards a tree by the wall.

"I know it's very old," replies her uncle. "The markings have worn away and you can see how the tree became bent as it grew up around it. Some people say it marks the grave of Ayr's last witch, but that can't be true. If someone was found guilty of witchcraft, it was because they were thought to worship the devil, so their remains would never have been buried in the hallowed ground by a church. It is a bit of a mystery though because back in the time when the church was here, it was unusual for people to use headstones. I think it was most likely put there by a local stone mason, perhaps to mark where his family were buried."

Martha is pretty sure she knows who that stone mason was. "There is certainly a lot of history in this town," she says, and her uncle nods in agreement.

* * * * * * *

Later that same day, Martha wakes up with a start. "Oh! Where am I? What year is it?" she blurts out, before quickly realising that she is in her aunt and uncle's car. Harry and Katie both burst out laughing.

"What was that about?" asks Katie through her giggles.

"Oh, nothing," says Martha, "I just fell asleep and woke up when the car stopped. I must have been dreaming."

"You were funny," Katie continues to snigger as she gets out of the car.

"Yeah, it was one of those silly, mixed-up dreams. I'd tell you about it, but I can't even remember it now." And Martha follows her sister out of the car and along a path to the shore.

But Martha has a lot on her mind and she would like to talk to someone about it. She wonders whether she should tell her sister about her time-travelling experiences. Can she trust Katie not to tell their aunt and uncle? Is her little sister capable of keeping a very big secret?

Usually Martha tells her friend Sarah everything that happens to her, but Sarah is on a family camping trip and still hasn't replied to the message Martha sent her yesterday afternoon. Martha decides that maybe she will talk to Katie, if it feels right and if Harry and her aunt and uncle aren't around.

They have parked close to a beach and they all throw some pebbles into the sea, trying to make them skim across the water. It doesn't take long before Katie asks, "Can I go for a swim?"

"Later," says Aunty Mary, "I've packed some towels in the car for when we get back, but first we're taking a walk along this beach. We're going to see a castle."

Along the way, they explore some tidal pools. In one of them, Martha spots a few tiny crabs and when her uncle lifts a large flat rock, there is a starfish hiding underneath. They take some photos and then continue along the beach until they find a place where there are steps that lead them up to the top of a cliff. Having reached the top there is a wonderful castle waiting for them. Not a ruin, but a complete, lived-in castle.

Just then, Martha's phone buzzes. At last! A text from Sarah:

> Still at campsite bad signal soz :(1652 is that ur history essay haven't started mine x

Martha frantically composes a text back:

> Not essay. I really time travelled to 1652

Another text from Sarah arrives:

> **Think ur dreaming**
> 😂 😂 x

Meanwhile, Aunty Mary is reading aloud from a guidebook, "Culzean Castle," she states, "was designed by the famous Scottish architect Robert Adam, son of Lord William Adam ..."

"Isn't that your surname, Uncle Porridge?" asks Katie. "Are you related to Lord William Adam?"

"Unfortunately, I don't think so," answers Uncle Porridge, "they were a very wealthy family."

"I don't think they were always wealthy," says Aunty Mary, "it says here that 'William Adam was the son of a stone mason, John Adam ...' It goes on a bit, let me see, yes, 'William married the daughter of a Lord' so that's probably when the family became wealthy."

Martha isn't listening to any of this. She is desperate to tell her best friend all about the extremely weird experience that has been happening to her, but it is impossible to do so by text. She tries to call Sarah, but again it goes to voice mail. She sends one more text:

> **Omg you need to call me!!**

"Sorry about that, Aunty Mary," says Martha and she puts her phone away. She knows she should have been listening to her aunt's description of the castle, but she is totally preoccupied with her thoughts about Johnny and his life in the 1650s.

There has been a conversation going on between Katie, Uncle Porridge and Aunty Mary, and now Martha finally tunes into it.

"Maybe Lord William was your grandfather?" suggests Katie.

"This was hundreds of years ago. How old do you think I am?! What year are we talking about Mary?"

Aunty Mary continues to refer to her guide book, "I've lost that page, let me see ... yes, John died in 1710, but his son William was born in 1689, Robert was born 3rd July 1728, he designed this castle and it was built between 1777 and 1792."

"Well maybe he was your great-grandfather," suggests Katie, "or your great-great-grandfather?"

"or your great-great-great-grandfather?" Harry joins in, "or your great-great-great-great-great-great-great-great-great ..."

"Enough of the 'greats'!" bellows Uncle Porridge. "Anyone for an ice-cream?"

"Can it be a great-great-great-great-great big ice-cream, please?" asks Harry.

Friday

XV

Present Day

Ding-dong, ding-dong, ding-dong, ding-dong, Martha wakes to the chime of church bells. She puts on her grubby slippers, and gives a fleeting look across to Katie and Harry in their beds. They are both fast asleep.

"My bells are calling me, I have to go," she whispers with a chuckle, and she scampers to the bathroom. She opens the window shutters just enough to see out. "YES," she hisses, and gives herself two thumbs up. The church is there.

The bells stop chiming, and Johnny saunters out of the church and strolls around in its grounds. Good. He doesn't seem to be in a hurry this morning. She closes the shutters and puts on the dressing gown.

Again today, Martha's heartbeat is jumping loudly, but it is pure excitement. She doesn't feel scared - well, maybe a little bit scared of meeting that horrible Maggie woman again, but not scared about getting home. She feels sure that when it is time for her to return to the present day, she will find a way back. She is not going to let any worries about one mean witchy person stop her from enjoying this incredible opportunity. She is the luckiest girl alive and she really wants to make the most of every moment of it.

She walks down the stairs, and once more the front door swings open before she reaches it. This time she doesn't hesitate at all. Martha skips straight outside and finds herself back in Johnny's time, the time of the big old church, and the time when Cromwell's soldiers were building a citadel in Ayr.

Martha

XVI

May 1652

Johnny looks up after removing a rabbit from its snare. "Good morning to ye, Martha," he says, but his voice isn't as bright and cheery as usual. "Ma mither said that Maggie Osborne was troubling ye yesterday. Did ye get hame safely?"

"I did, thanks," says Martha.

"Maggie was ootside when I got home. She couldna unnerstand how ye went away withoot her seeing ye."

"She thinks I'm a witch," laughs Martha.

"If ye are, then ye're the bonniest witch there ever was. But witchcraft is wrang. Ye do ken that Martha?

"I'm not a witch, Johnny."

"It's dangerous fir yer soul and ye must have heard aboot the women who cast up evil spirits and were burned at the stake fir it."

"I'm not a witch, I promise. I ...," Martha doesn't want to lie to Johnny, so she chooses her words carefully. "I slipped out of your house while your mother was asleep and while Maggie was busy scratching at fleas. Honestly it's true." She stands in front of him and waits for his response.

"I'm sorry, Martha. Forgive me. I shouldna have asked," he eventually utters, obviously relieved.

Martha is relieved too. When she first met Johnny, she thought he would think her crazy if she told him where she actually comes from, so she decided to skip over the truth. Since then, she has been careful in everything she says and does so that she appears to be a normal girl, just a bit different because she comes from a different part of the country. Now that she knows Johnny better, she would love to share her real story with him, but sadly she realises she can't. He would think her a witch. She decides to change the subject, and asks, "How's your mother?"

"She's much better. The herbs and the ginger and the salt aw seem to be helping. Thank ye Martha."

Martha wonders if she has been travelling to this time purely to heal Johnny's mother. If so, it looks like her job was completed quite simply. Johnny interrupts her thoughts, "Will ye help me look fir the rabbits in ma snares?"

"Okay," she replies.

"Was that 'och aye'?"

"It was, okay. Yes, aye!"

* * * * * * *

Together they collect four rabbits. Johnny takes a knife from his pocket and makes a slit in the back leg of one of the rabbits. He then takes the other back foot and pushes it through the hole he just made. He does the same with the next rabbit, but he puts one of the legs of the new rabbit, between the legs of the first rabbit and continues with all the rabbits until he has formed a chain with all the back legs. Martha watches fascinated. Daisy chains will never be the same after watching this. "We just need a stick noo," Johnny informs her.

They find an old fallen branch near a clump of trees by the church, and Johnny snaps off a smaller branch and uses his knife to strip away the leaves. He pokes this stick through the chain of rabbit legs, so that the rabbits can hang from it. They lift up this strange package, place it on their shoulders and carry it, one behind the other, all the way to the High Street.

At the Fish Cross, a woman with two young girls is selling fish from a large basket. They are wearing plain dresses with aprons, and Martha notices that the mother has laced boots, but her daughters are barefoot. Johnny speaks to the woman, trades two of the rabbits for four fish and hands her a piece of cloth from his pocket to wrap them in. Johnny tells Martha that he'll trade or sell the other rabbits at the market tomorrow. He has saved up some money and hopes to buy his first stone carving tool.

They chat about the weekly market and Johnny tells Martha that, when the traders come, there are stalls and carts selling grain and vegetables and all sorts of useful goods. They also have a sheep market, a wool market and a market for horses and cattle further along the High Street.

Before long, Johnny says that he must go and join his father building the big wall. He asks Martha if she will take the other rabbits and the fish to his house, and she says she'd be happy to.

"Will I see ye the morn?" he asks.

"I hope so," she says. "We leave for home on Sunday, so tomorrow will probably be my last chance to see you."

"Till the morn!" and Johnny tips his cap slightly.

* * * * * * *

When Martha reaches Johnny's house, she meets his mother at the doorstep. Mrs Adam is sweeping out the dusty floor with a broom, and is obviously feeling a lot better. She is pleased to see Martha again and delighted with the fish. "Would ye like to have yer tea wi' us the day, Martha?" she asks.

"No, I need to go home to my family."

Martha hears some loud bangs. "What's that noise?"

"That'll be the sojers, probably using the kirk fir target practice again."

"Oh, I'd like to go along and see that," says Martha, remembering the marks Uncle Porridge showed her on the side of the tower, and how he said they had been caused by musket fire.

"In that case, please will ye take this fish to oor neebor, Mrs Craig. She lives in the end cottage."

"Can I pop back later?"

"Pop?"

"Can I come back later?"

"Aye, onytime ma dear," and they say goodbye.

* * * * * * *

Martha walks along the lane till she reaches the end cottage. She knocks on the door and introduces herself. Mrs Craig thanks her for delivering the fish and Martha retraces her steps along the lane and walks towards the grounds of the church.

The musket fire is very loud. Whenever there is a pause in the firing, a short, fat soldier comes out of the church and hollers instructions in a loud, gruff voice. He then goes back into the church and the firing starts again. The soldiers are firing from a position on the harbour side of the church, and Martha pictures them standing on the tennis courts in her modern day life. She is approaching a raised circular wall, quite close to the church, when a strong hand lands on her shoulder and pushes her down into a crouch.

"Watch out Miss, you'll get yourself killed. Take cover here by the well." A very smart looking soldier in a red coat crouches down next to her. His voice was strict, but he has a kind-looking face, and Martha understands that he is concerned for her safety.

"This is no place to be when Sergeant Norfolk is conducting target practice. Our men aren't the best of aims! But good-oh, the sergeant's taking a quick break, follow me!" and he leads Martha into the church porch. Then he stands back and takes a look at her. "I recognise you from a couple of mornings ago when I was surveying the land for the new barracks. You looked lost then," he says, "are you lost now?"

"No, I'm just exploring."

"Where do you live?"

"I live in Wiltshire," she says. Martha knows from her history lessons that Cromwell's soldiers are from England, so she wonders if this man might have heard of Wiltshire. He looks astonished.

"You are a long way from home," he says.

"I'm visiting my aunt and uncle here in Ayr."

"Well I never. A young lady from Wiltshire. What's your name?"

"Martha."

"Miss Martha. Let me introduce myself. My name is Major Talbot. I don't suppose you've ever visited the village of Lacock in Wiltshire? I was there not so long ago to see ..."

"Yes, I know Lacock," Martha interrupts, "we went to Lacock Abbey for a picnic last summer. My sister Katie loved swimming in the river there."

"Yes, it is a splendid place," and he appears to ponder a pleasant memory for a moment or two before turning his attention back to Martha. "Well, for now you must keep safe. Stay in the church until Sergeant Norfolk tells us that he has finished drilling the platoon in musket fire," and Major Talbot guides Martha inside.

"Can I look around?" she asks.

"Yes," he nods, "but please don't touch anything."

It is a large church, but Martha quickly finds the spiral staircase that takes her up to the top of the tower and onto the parapet. She goes outside to look at the view. It is amazing. The whole big church is set out below her, and she spots Johnny's home in the row of six stone cottages on the edge of the town.

She sees the tents that some of the army are using for temporary homes and the wide open space where she ran about, bewildered, on Wednesday morning. Wooden posts have been knocked into the ground, marking out the shape of a huge hexagon, and she realises it must be the outline of the citadel to be built. Some foundations have been dug for the soldiers' barracks and several men are busy working on the citadel wall near the harbour.

She gazes out across the town. It is much, much smaller than when she looked at it from the tower with her family on Monday and she stares hard, trying to take a snapshot of it in her mind. She follows the track of the river from behind the town along to the harbour and notices that there is only one bridge across it, and then she glances out to sea.

The Isle of Arran is there of course in the distance, but in front of it there is a beautiful square-rigged sailing ship floating across the bay. It looks wonderful. "Whoo hoo!" she yells, punching her fist in the air, but the firing starts again so she quickly ducks down and makes her way back to the stairs.

On her way down, Martha stops at each floor to look in the rooms. The top floor is stocked with sacks of grain and other foodstuff; dead pheasants and pigs are hanging from a beam. There are also two bells, high up in the rafters. They are bronze coloured and one is bigger than the other. Martha sees that each bell is attached to a wooden wheel with a rope dangling from it. The ropes drop straight down until they disappear through a hole in the floor. The chiming of these bells has provided her wake-up call each morning. She nods a thank you to them. "Are you magic bells?" she asks, but there is no reply.

On the next floor Martha comes across an elderly man. He is wearing a black cloak and is sat writing at a desk that is covered in paperwork. Behind him there are dusty boxes of books, candles and candlesticks, and Martha notices church robes hanging on hooks around the room. She says hello to the man and he introduces himself as Mr Hamilton, and he asks Martha if he can help her with anything. She thanks him, but says she is just visiting the area and exploring. He tells her that he is doing the accounts for the church and for the school, and it is a bigger job than ever since the soldiers moved into the church. He smiles and whispers to Martha that he will need to send a big bill to Oliver Cromwell to pay for all the upheaval.

"Are you from the Blackfriar's monastery?" Martha asks him.

"Na," he answers, "the friaries in Ayr closed a lang time ago. I used to teach in the school, but noo I help the minister to look after the kirk."

"Did you ever teach a boy called Johnny ... Johnny Adam?" she asks.

"Oh! So ye're a friend o' Johnny's are ye?" and he beams at her. "Whit's yer name?"

"Martha."

"Well, I'm very pleased to meet ye, Martha. Johnny and I are firm friends too."

Martha continues down the stairs, and she discovers that the room on the next floor is stacked high with an assortment of military treasures that she knows Harry and Uncle Porridge would love to see: piles of armour, helmets, swords and muskets, plus wooden boxes that she thinks are full of ammunition. And she spots scrolls of paper, covered with fancy lettering, poking out of a tall cubbyhole.

On the floor below, Martha pauses at the doorway. When she made her way up the tower, this room had been empty, but since then it has filled with people. She rests against the doorframe for a few minutes, watching the goings on.

A couple of soldiers are leaning over a table, sketching plans onto a large map of the town. Other soldiers are sitting on the seats in the alcoves, some holding clay bottles, others with goblets, all chatting boisterously. She sees the big fireplace where she stood with her brother and sister on Monday. There is a fire burning there now, with a large cooking pot simmering on a rack above it. Martha has to walk across this room to continue down the stairs, and she feels a little nervous as she enters it, but nobody looks up. They are all busy with their own activities.

Martha reaches the ground floor of the tower. It is much calmer here, and she is slightly startled by something brushing against her shoulder. The *something* is two dangling ropes and her eyes follow them up to a hole in the ceiling, up to her bells in the rafters.

She enters the main part of the church, and her eyes are drawn to the magnificent stained glass window ahead of her. Sunlight is pouring through, scattering pretty colours all over the stone floor and across the wooden seats. Two ladies are praying and a few soldiers are resting, while some others are talking quietly to each other. The cracking sounds of musket fire continue, and Martha takes a seat on one of the pews.

She wonders if time is passing at the same rate here as it is for her family in present day Ayr. It was soon after sunrise when she left, and everyone was asleep, so she doesn't think she will be missed yet. But she can't risk being away for too long. At least she has a good plan for getting home. The chair in Johnny's house took her safely home yesterday; hopefully it will do the same again today.

She thinks about the chair. Perhaps it works like the TARDIS, from 'Dr. Who'? If only she could learn how to control it, then maybe she could travel back to 1652 whenever she wants, instead of having to wait for the church bells to chime each morning.

She wishes she could go straight to that special chair now, but Major Talbot told her to stay put until the shooting practise has finished, and he is still in the church. He is conferring with a couple of soldiers by the porch, so for the time being, she can't even sneak past him. Occasionally there is a short pause in the firing, but it soon starts up again. She will just have to sit it out and wait.

There are some books dotted around the pews. The first she picks up is a black prayer book, but it's in Latin and she can't read the text. The next is a dark brown book of psalms and hymns, and it's in English. Martha flicks through it, seeking out verses that she recognises; meanwhile, hoping and praying that the musket firing will cease completely, so that she can go back to Johnny's house and, from there, return home to her family.

It is surprisingly warm inside the church, out of the breeze; quite stuffy with the smell of soldiers, to-ing and fro-ing about their business. Martha's eyelids grow heavy and she puts the book down. It was another early start for her this morning and she is very tired.

XVII

Present Day

Martha jolts awake. She is still sitting on the same pew, but everything else is different. The book on the pew in front of her is now a modern, white hymnal. She is in a church, but it is a different shape and it has upper levels with balconies. In front of her there is an ornate, dark wooden pulpit with organ pipes above. The huge, colourful window has gone, but Martha looks around and spots several smaller, stained glass windows, mostly in arch-shaped pairs. Thankfully, there is no sound of musket fire and there are no soldiers to be seen. Martha is certain that this is not the church she entered.

She initially thinks she is alone, but then she hears a woman's voice, humming to the tune of "All Things Bright and Beautiful," and she notices a lady arranging flowers in vases in a porch at the back of the church. The best news is that behind the porch there is an open door leading to a churchyard. Martha wastes no time in hurrying towards it.

"Excuse me," she says to the lady as she strides past her and through the door.

"Oh my dear! Whatever are you doing out in your dressing gown and slippers?" the lady calls after her.

"Sorry! Bye!" shouts Martha, she has no time to hang around and chat. Once outside, a quick look around tells her that she is in the grounds of the Auld Kirk that she visited with her uncle yesterday. "Phew!" she lets out a gasp of relief, "I'll have to be careful where I fall asleep in the 17th century. I could wake up anywhere!"

Martha scuttles along the High Street, feeling a little foolish to be out in her night clothes. Fortunately it is still quite early, the shops aren't open yet and she passes very few people. It's kind of funny, she thinks, how wearing her dressing gown outside doesn't seem to matter so much in Johnny's time. There, she would probably feel more out of place in her jeans.

Martha reaches the tower grounds and wonders what time it is. How long has she been away? She approaches her aunt and uncle's house and notices that the front door is open. Aunty Mary is out on the pavement with her back to Martha, talking to another lady who is standing in a garden a couple of doors along. Martha looks up to the bathroom window and sees that the window shutters are still closed. Good, her aunt can't have been up long and everyone else is probably still in bed.

Martha is currently hidden by a hedge, so she picks her moment to make a dash through the gate, but she knocks against it and the hinge squeaks. Martha just reaches the porch as Aunty Mary turns around. "Oh, good morning, Martha, I thought I heard someone there. I'm talking to Pamela, she's the organiser of the pageant tomorrow."

Martha quickly stops moving. Luckily, it seems like her aunt thinks she has just come downstairs and wandered out onto the doorstep. The hedge probably kept her hidden from Pamela too. She waves and calls, "Hi! I'm Martha. What's a pageant?"

"A play," answers her aunt. "Remember I told you there's going to be an outdoor performance at the tower tomorrow. Pamela would love for the three of you to be involved."

"Yes," says Pamela, "the pageant starts at three, but I need you to come over to the tower at ten tomorrow morning. We're having a run through of everything and I'll get you all sorted out with costumes."

* * * * * * *

After breakfast, Aunty Mary takes Martha, Katie and Harry to the village of Alloway. They visit Burn's Cottage and learn that Robert Burns was a famous Scottish poet who lived in the 1700s.

"You know the Scottish poems that Uncle Porridge tells us? Were they written here?" asks Katie.

"This is where the poet who wrote them was born, but he moved away when he was older," replies her aunt.

"It's just like Johnny's house," says Martha, looking around and reminding herself that she is in the present day and not in the midst of one of her time travel episodes.

"Who's Johnny?" asks Katie.

"Sorry, I didn't mean to say that out loud," Martha replies, "you don't know him."

"Oh, okay," says Katie. She used to know all of Martha's friends, but that changed when her big sister started secondary school. "But he lives in a house like this?" she persists.

"Kind of, yeah, although his is smaller. It only has two proper rooms and a small out-house."

"Really? But he must have electricity."

"Actually, no, he doesn't."

"Wow!" says Katie, completely astonished. "So he doesn't have a TV?"

"Nope."

"What about lights?"

"His family use candles and oil lamps."

"How does he charge his phone?"

"He doesn't have a phone. Even if he had a phone, I don't think it would work."

"How come?"

Martha thinks carefully about her answer. "He doesn't have a signal where he lives."

"Oh. Does he mind?"

Martha wonders about this. Johnny is so chatty and busy all the time. How could he possibly mind not having something that he doesn't even know exists? "No, he doesn't grumble about stuff."

"He sounds interesting," interrupts Aunty Mary.

"I'd like to meet him," says Katie, "you should ask Mum if you can invite him home one day."

"Uh ... maybe," says Martha, then smartly changing the subject she holds out her phone and asks, "Aunty Mary, please can you take a photo of Katie and me standing here by this old fireplace?"

Martha poses with Katie, but she is thinking about Johnny's life with no television and no phone. She wonders if he has any photos. She plans to put her phone in the dressing gown pocket so she can take his photo tomorrow morning.

They continue walking around Burn's cottage, but Harry starts bouncing a ball on the stone floor so Aunty Mary takes him into the garden to play catch while Martha and Katie remain inside.

Martha notices the canopy over a bed and remembers seeing the same thing in Johnny's house. She reads on an information card that beds often had curtains to keep the draughts out and canopies 'to catch bugs that dropped out of the thatched roof at night. She wonders if that is why princesses had four-poster beds in storybooks too. Being a fairy-tale princess wasn't as glamorous as she'd been led to believe.

"Does your friend Johnny have carpets?" asks Katie.

"No, his house is really basic. I think it's just a dirt floor."

Martha realises that Katie is quite fascinated about Johnny and his home; she would be amazed to visit Johnny's house for real. Martha doesn't share much of her life with her little sister anymore, and again she considers sharing the secret of her early morning adventures. Martha knows she can't include any adults in her time travels, but maybe she can include Katie. Maybe she should risk telling her sister, or better still, maybe tomorrow she will take Katie with her.

Saturday

XVIII

Present Day

Ding-dong, ding-dong, ding-dong, ding-dong, Martha wakes to the chime of church bells. "Yes!" she says, sitting up quickly and glancing over to Katie's bed. "Katie! Katie, wake up!" she whispers as loudly as she dares, and she looks over at Harry in the corner of the room. He is dangling half out of his bed again this morning and fortunately seems to be soundly asleep. Martha doesn't want to waken her little brother, so she leans over close to Katie and gently shakes her shoulder. Her sister stirs.

"What is it?" Katie blurts out.

"Shsh!" says Martha, "I've got something to show you. Quickly, put your slippers on and grab your cardigan, we're going outside."

"Really? Why?"

"I told you, I've got something to show you." Martha is about to take Katie straight downstairs, but she decides they should probably both use the bathroom first. It will also allow her to show Katie the view of the church from the bathroom window and explain what to expect before they head out. She doesn't want to be trying to answer a ton of questions outside, in 1652, if Maggie Osborne is hanging around.

She grabs the dressing gown from the back of the door and checks the pocket. Good, she remembered to put her phone there last night. She doesn't plan to take many photos, just one of the church, one of Johnny, one of the view from the top of the tower and one with some soldiers in it. Of course it would be good to get one of the men building the citadel wall and perhaps a photo of the fishing boats at the harbour too. She takes a deep breath and opens the window shutters.

She sees the tower, but only the tower. She shuts the shutters and opens them again, but nothing changes. The church isn't there and her heart sinks.

"Oh no! That's not fair. Katie, you ruin everything!" She feels so cross. The bells called her and she had a chance to go back to the time of the old church again. It was another chance to see Johnny and learn more about his life, but she messed it up. The bells didn't wake Katie. She should have realised that the bells are her own special bells. How could she have been so foolish as to try to include her sister? "Just go back to bed!" she snaps.

"What?" says Katie, "what have I done?!" She has been dragged out of bed and into the bathroom for some unknown reason, and now her big sister is telling her off. Tears well up in her eyes and she clenches her hands into fists. "You're mean, Martha and you're weird." She turns to stomp off back to bed, but Martha catches her hand and pulls her back.

"No Katie, don't go. I'm sorry, I didn't mean it. It's not your fault. I just wanted to show you something, it should have been really special. I thought it would happen this morning, but it hasn't. I'm sorry," and Martha desperately tries to put aside her own disappointment.

Katie sighs. She doesn't know what's going on, and her big sister has definitely been acting strange, but she has said sorry so there is no point in sulking about it. "Well what did you want to show me?" she asks.

"Maybe I'll get another chance to show you," says Martha, although secretly she knows that if the church is there tomorrow morning there is absolutely no way she will risk trying to show it to Katie or anyone. Tomorrow will be her last morning in Scotland, and it could be the last chance she ever has to see Johnny again.

"Do you want to go back to bed because we could play a game? Or, I'll take you to the beach if you want to go for a swim or ..." Martha thinks hard, "we could go to the kitchen and make pancakes?"

Katie's eyes light up at this last suggestion. "Pancakes would be good!" she nods and smiles.

* * * * * * *

Just before ten o'clock, Aunty Mary walks the children over to the tower where they meet up with Pamela and a bunch of local kids. Pamela shoos Aunty Mary away along with all the other parents who are hanging around. "You will all see the grand performance this afternoon!" she tells them.

Once everyone who is taking part in the pageant has arrived, Pamela explains to the children that the story is set in the 1650s when Oliver Cromwell's soldiers arrived in Ayr and built Cromwell's Citadel. This is decidedly spooky for Martha, and she has to force herself to concentrate on listening to Pamela rather than thinking about her own encounter with the 1650s.

"Our actors, actresses and musicians have all been rehearsing for several weeks," Pamela tells them. "It's quite a long play, but don't worry, there aren't any difficult lines for you to learn. You do need to move around at different times and so you need to know where to go and when to stand and when to sit, actually, you know what? I think it will be easiest if we just run through it."

"It starts with everyone inside the tower," Pamela continues, "so, children, can you please go up to the second floor and wait for me there. Town people and soldiers, I want you on the first floor. Musicians, wait on the ground floor until I tell you to start the procession. Okay, let's move!"

They run through the play. The musicians exit the tower first, playing their instruments as they walk along. The adult actors and actresses exit next and then the dozen or more children taking part follow behind. They all walk in a procession around the tower and around the area where the audience will be sitting. Harry is given a long pole with a flag to carry and Katie and Martha both think he looks very cute.

During most of the play, the children sit together on some benches, but there are key points during the performance when they have to remember to stand up and curtsey or bow to one of the actors. At other times they have to boo or cheer or repeat a phrase that someone else says first. They don't have any lines to remember on their own, so it is all fairly straightforward.

They finish rehearsing and Pamela takes the children back up to the second floor of the tower to sort out their costumes. There are two rails full of clothes and a box with hats, shoes and boots. Harry is a little disappointed that he has to wear a peasant boy's costume. He really wanted to be a soldier, but he has some fun with the other boys, trying on raggedy trousers, shirts, waistcoats and cloaks.

Martha finds a flat cap in the hat box and plonks it on Harry's head. It makes him look like he could be a little brother to Johnny. For a moment, Martha feels annoyed with herself as she remembers that she missed her chance to visit Johnny this morning. She hopes the bells will call her one more time so that she has a chance to say goodbye to her friend.

She turns her attention to the rail of girls' clothes. There are old-fashioned skirts, smock tops and dresses for the girls to try, plus an assortment of aprons, pinafores and capes to put on top. They each have to wear a white cotton bonnet with their hair tucked up inside. Martha, Katie and the other girls all find good outfits to wear, except Martha can't find any old-fashioned footwear in her size.

"It doesn't matter," says Pamela, "your skirt comes to the floor, so I don't think anyone will notice. Or if you want, you could go barefoot. Most children wouldn't have had shoes in the 17th century." Pamela tells the children to keep their costumes on and sends them home for lunch. "Be back by two-thirty!" she tells them.

* * * * * * *

"Can we light a fire in our room tonight?" Martha asks her aunt as they are finishing their lunch. "I've been thinking all week that it would be nice to toast some marshmallows there."

"I like the sound of that," says Aunty Mary. "Why don't you and Katie run over to the sweet shop now? Your mum and dad will be here soon, and we'll follow over with Harry and meet you at the tower. This week has flown by so fast. I can't believe you're going home tomorrow."

Aunty Mary gives the girls some money and they walk to the shop. Martha buys two large packets of marshmallows and stuffs them in her pockets. Katie asks the shopkeeper if he has any traditional Scottish sweets, and he recommends tablet.

"It looks like fudge," Katie says.

"But tastes much better," says the shopkeeper.

They buy two slabs and Katie tucks them in her pockets. They return to the tower and look for the family. Uncle Porridge soon arrives with Harry. "Your aunt is still waiting for your mum and dad," he tells them, "but your mum just texted to say they're nearly here."

Pamela ushers the children into the tower, and they wait with the other kids on the second floor. In due course, Pamela says it is time for the play to begin, and they line up in the room. They hear the musicians commencing two floors below them, and they start to make their way down the spiral staircase. Martha is at the back of the line.

They reach the first floor and cross the room to continue down the last flight of steps. Martha hears the music playing as it did at the rehearsal, but she also hears bells chiming, *ding-dong, ding-dong, ding-dong, ding-dong, ding-dong* … The bells get louder and louder and as Martha reaches the ground floor, she can't hear the music for the pageant anymore. All she can hear is the sound of the church bells calling her.

XIX

May 1652

Martha steps out of the tower, but she is not in the grounds of the tower. She finds herself in the back of the old church. "Wow! That was cool, I wasn't expecting that!" she exclaims.

Mr Hamilton is standing nearby. "Hello Martha. Sorry, did I startle ye wi' the din of the bells?"

"No, no, well, yes. Yes, actually it was a bit of a surprise," says Martha. "Is a service about to begin?"

"Na, we were just changing the ropes," says Mr Hamilton, busily coiling up a long length of rope and putting it in a sack. "Johnny was helping me, and he rang the bells to check they work properly, but he's left the noo. Ye've just missed him."

"Do you know where he went?" Martha asks.

Mr Hamilton starts to answer, but Major Talbot comes down the stairs, steps out of the tower and almost bumps into Martha. "Oh hello, Miss Martha, I didn't know you were here. Not lost again are you?! You should take a look at this," and the major chortles as he unravels a large scroll of paper that he is carrying under his arm.

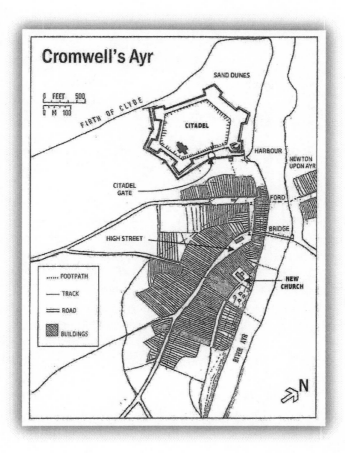

Martha sees that it is a map of Ayr showing the citadel and the new church to be built.

"Hopefully it will be finished when you next visit Ayr," continues Major Talbot. "It's going to be quite splendid, but we don't want our visitors getting lost. Is there something I can help you with today?"

"No, thank you, I'm uh, just looking for a friend," she stammers.

"Most people are at the market, have you tried there?"

"I will. Thank you, Major Talbot," she says. "Bye for now and goodbye, Mr Hamilton."

* * * * * * *

Martha thinks that Johnny probably is at the market, but she wants to call by his house first to see how his mother is and say goodbye to her.

She walks to the cottage and knocks at Johnny's door. There is no response. She tries again and still there is no response, but just as she is leaving, she hears a noise coming from inside. Martha puts her ear up to the door. It sounds like someone moaning. She calls out, "Hello, anyone home?" as she opens the door and goes in.

On entering, Martha shockingly sees that someone is slumped on the floor in a puddle of water. She realises that it is Johnny's mother. She rushes over and bends down next to her saying, "Mrs Adam! Mrs Adam, what happened?"

Mrs Adam opens her eyes, "Martha, please, I need help," and she shuts her eyes again.

Martha is knocked for six. How can she get help when there are no phones, no doctors and no ambulances? Then she remembers Johnny saying that his neighbour, Mrs Craig, came to help when his baby sister was born last year. Martha takes hold of Mrs Adam's hand and gives it a tight squeeze, "I'll be right back," she says.

Martha leaves the house and runs straight to the end of the lane. She skids on the dirt track, stopping right outside Mrs Craig's home and she desperately batters on the door.

"Whit's aw the clatter?!" comes a voice from within as the door swings open.

"Oh Mrs Craig, I'm so pleased you're home. It's Mrs Adam. She needs help. I think ... I think it could be the baby ... the wean."

"Just haud on," says Mrs Craig. She goes back inside and then reappears with a bundle of linen, which she plonks into Martha's arms. "Right noo, let's be off."

They hurry along to Johnny's house and arrive to find that Mrs Adam is still on the floor. Mrs Craig starts talking straight away, "Ena, I'm here. Ye're gaun to be fine dear. Martha, help me take Mrs Adam through to the bedroom. We'll have mair room there than wi' the wee box-bed."

Together, they help Mrs Adam to her feet and take her through to a bed in the second room. "Noo Martha, put some water on to heat and take that empty bucket and go fill it up at the well, then come straight back. I'm gaun to need yer help."

For a few seconds, Martha stands still in shock. Mrs Adam is about to have her baby and Mrs Craig is expecting her to help and she doesn't even know where the well is. She hears a cry of, "Make haste, lass!" and immediately jumps into action.

She remembers how Johnny had roused the fire and hung the kettle over it, so she checks there is water in the kettle and puts it in position. She adds some wood to the hearth and riddles the fire with the poker, and then she thinks about the well. Somebody mentioned a well recently. Yes, she remembers, Major Talbot told her to take cover by the well near the church. She grabs the bucket and charges out to fill it up and hurry back.

When Martha returns, Mrs Craig is washing her hands in a basin of warm water. She rips up a strip of linen and instructs Martha to dip it in the icy water from the well and use it to cool Mrs Adam's forehead. "Mrs Adam is suffering," she tells Martha, "the wean is roond the wrang way. It's gaun to need ma help to be born. Mrs Adam keeps fainting and that isnae good. I need ye to haud her haun and keep talking. Ye must keep her awake."

"What shall I talk about?" asks Martha.

"Onything, Martha. It doesnae matter. Just gie her yer haun to haud and try to keep her mind off the pain."

So Martha holds Mrs Adam's hand and she starts to talk. She tells her a story about a girl who lives hundreds of years in the future. She talks about the girl's family, her sister and her brother, the school she goes to and her friends at school, and Mrs Craig says, "That's good, keep gaun lass."

So Martha talks about the things that the girl has in the future, like carriages called cars that don't need horses to pull them and can travel ten miles in ten minutes; and big machines called aeroplanes that fly in the sky like birds and can carry over a hundred people to England in an hour.

Every now and then Mrs Craig says, "Deep breaths, Ena," and then she looks at Martha and again says, "keep gaun lass." So Martha talks about telephones and televisions and computers and microwave ovens that can bake a potato in just a few minutes. She tells Mrs Adam that in the future most women go to hospitals or special maternity units to have their babies. She explains that there are doctors and nurses at the hospitals, to help people, and they have lots of different medicine for if you are sick, and Martha realises how lucky she is to live in a time with all these amazing things. She keeps talking and talking and, all the while, Martha holds Mrs Adam's hand.

Sometimes Mrs Adam is obviously in a lot of pain, and she squeezes hard on Martha's hand, but eventually Martha hears Mrs Craig saying, "That's good, Ena, here we are noo," and Martha hears a gurgle and a wail and she sees that Mrs Craig is holding up a tiny, squishy, slippery looking little baby by its feet.

Mrs Adam gasps, "It's a boy?"

"Aye," says Mrs Craig, "and he looks a good strong lad to me." Mrs Craig asks Martha to pass her a clean piece of linen and she wraps the baby up and hands him to Mrs Adam. Mrs Adam is in tears, and Mrs Craig is in tears, and Martha starts to fill up too. They are all quiet for a few minutes as Mrs Adam nurses her baby, then Mrs Craig says, "That was some wonderful story, Martha! Ye've got a lively imagination!"

"Ye stopped me from thinkin' aboot the pain," says Mrs Adam, "thank ye, Martha."

"What will you call the baby?" Martha asks.

"I like the name, Iain," says Mrs Adam.

"Ye cannae call him Iain," says Mrs Craig, "ye already have a Johnny. Iain is the same name as John in the Gaelic."

"Well, let's see whit his faither wants to call him," says Mrs Adam.

"Martha, do ye want to run and fetch Mr Adam and Johnny?" Mrs Craig suggests.

"You bet! Will they be at the market?"

"Na, I saw Johnny there this morning. Ye'll probably find the both o' them at the big waw."

* * * * * * *

111

Martha sprints to the harbour. She sees a group of men, working near the citadel wall, and as she approaches them she calls out, "Mr Adam? Johnny?"

The men are hammering pins into large chunks of rock, breaking them into smaller pieces. It is noisy work, but one of the men hears Martha's call and looks around. "Try along there," he suggests, pointing to a section of the wall where a corner is being constructed.

Martha dashes on and quickly spots Johnny's father. "Mr Adam!" she breathlessly calls, but he keeps talking to one of the soldiers while chalking numbers on the wall. Johnny is sitting nearby, cleaning some tools, and he looks up at Martha. Some of the other men stop working and look around. "Mr Adam!" she tries again. This time he stops talking and turns to look at Martha.

"Aye, whit is it lass?"

"Do you want to come and meet your new son?!" she gasps, beaming. All the men give a loud cheer and Mr Adam, Johnny and Martha all run back to Johnny's house together.

* * * * * * *

Martha stands by the doorway of the bedroom, allowing Johnny and his father to stride ahead to the top of the bed where Johnny's mother is sitting up, nursing the new baby. "Is it really true?" pants Mr Adam. His wife looks up, nods and smiles at him. "Thanks be to God," he declares, before leaning down to embrace his wife.

"Here," she says, handing the baby to Mr Adam, who cuddles his new son and then passes the bundle to Johnny.

"Whit shall we name him?" asks Mrs Adam.

"I was thinkin o' Peter," he says, looking hopefully at his wife, who smiles and nods again. "I like that name," she says.

"Aye, that's a good name," says Mrs Craig. "Peter means rock and he does seem to be a solid wee wan."

"And rock is important to oor family," says Johnny. "Wan day, he'll be my apprentice stone mason!" He turns to Martha. "Would ye like to haud ma wee brother?" he asks. She carefully takes the baby in her arms and cuddles him for a little while before handing him back to his mother.

"Were ye here fir lang?" Johnny asks Martha. She nods.

"It was Martha who found me in a heap on the floor," Mrs Adam informs him.

"And you fetched Mrs Craig?"

"Aye," says Martha.

Johnny throws his arms around Martha's waist, then picks her up and swings her round, cheering as he does so until Mrs Craig says, "Enough, noo! Let's gie yer mither and faither some quiet time," and she steers the children outside and returns to her own house.

Johnny and Martha sit together on the front doorstep, both happy and smiling. "Ye've got new clothes," Johnny observes as Martha pulls her skirt down over her ankles, wishing she had gone barefoot for the pageant, and carefully trying to hide her white hi-tops. She fails.

"And look at yer boots!" he says, "I've never seen onything like 'em. How do they feel?"

"Good. Do you want to try them on? We could swap?" Martha removes one shoe and Johnny pulls off a dirty leather boot and tries to squeeze his foot into Martha's trainer. It's too small.

"I'd only have got them durtie onyway," he says, handing the shoe back to her and putting his own back on.

"That's a shame," she says, "I'm going back to England tomorrow. It would have been nice to give you something to remember me by."

"I dinna think I'll ever forget ye Martha, dinna fret aboot that," and Johnny asks her if she will be back some day. Martha says she doesn't know, but she hopes so. "Well it's been right braw meeting ye," he tells her.

"It's been right braw meeting ye too, Johnny!" and she flings her arm around his shoulders and gives him a squeeze. As she does so, she notices the bulge in her pocket and remembers her plan to take some photos. Disappointingly though, Martha realises she has left her phone in the dressing gown pocket. Oh well, she'll just have to sketch some pictures instead, and on the bright side, she does have two bags of sweets in her skirt pockets.

"Look I've got something special here," she says. "I bought it ... uh ... back where I come from. I bet you've never seen anything like this before." She opens the bag and removes a pink marshmallow and passes it to Johnny.

Johnny squishes it. "Whit should I do wi' this?" he asks.

"Eat it," she says and she takes another from the bag and pops it in her mouth.

Johnny squeezes the sweet again, sniffs it, bites half of it off and warily sucks the strange item on his tongue for a few seconds before finally starting to chew. "I like that!" he announces and places the rest of the marshmallow in his mouth.

They sit munching on marshmallows and chatting. Johnny tells Martha that he has never met anyone like her before. "Ye're very different frae the lasses who live here."

"Where I come from I'm just an ordinary girl, nothing special. Although I do feel quite special now that I've met you."

Martha suddenly wonders what the time is and how long she has been there. She stands to leave. "I better go now. My family might be looking for me." Then, pulling the second pack of marshmallows from her pocket and passing them to Johnny, she says: "Here, take these too. You've got to try putting one on the end of a poker and holding it over the fire. They're right braw toasted!"

He stands up, "Farewell, Martha. I hope we'll meet again wan day."

Martha feels sad and she doesn't want to leave feeling like that. Johnny has a new baby brother, they should be celebrating. "Before I go, you've got to try something," she says, "copy me!" and she takes a marshmallow from the remains of the first pack and holds it towards her mouth.

"I dinna think I could eat any mair of them right noo," says Johnny, pulling a grimace and rubbing his stomach.

"You don't have to eat it," she says. "Just copy me, tuck it in your cheek."

Johnny copies Martha with one marshmallow, but she continues to put another sweet and then another into the sides of her mouth. Her cheeks start to puff out. She keeps tucking more and more in, and Johnny just stands and watches and shakes his head and starts giggling. Eventually Martha's cheeks are bulging absolutely full. She takes one more marshmallow and tries to push it into her mouth, but Johnny is already laughing at her so much that she can't keep a straight face. Martha splutters and guffaws and all the pink and white bouncy blobs shoot high, up and out of her mouth like a fountain.

"I will never forget ye noo," he laughs. They hug and say goodbye, and Johnny goes into his house.

* * * * * * *

Martha decides to return to the church. She is fairly sure she will be able to use one of the pews to take her home to the present day. She sets off, but hears a familiar irritating voice coming from behind just as a hand seizes her wrist.

"Did ye see thae balls o' pink and white frothing up oot o' her mooth, Sergeant Norfolk? This is the lass I told ye aboot. She's up to nae good."

Martha turns around. As she suspects, the woman holding her wrist is Maggie Osborne, and today she is not alone. She has the sergeant with her. He is hanging onto Maggie's other arm, and he seems also to be hanging onto Maggie's every word.

"Yes, yes, I did see," splutters Sergeant Norfolk, pulling himself up to his fullest height, which is not much taller than Martha. "So, this is the girl that's been bothering you?" he speaks in a commanding voice, clearly wanting to impress Maggie. "This is the girl who makes salt and fresh herbs appear from nowhere."

"Aye!" claims Maggie, "she's a witch, I tell ye, a witch! And just look at her fancy wee shoes!" Maggie lets go of Martha's wrist and grabs Martha's skirt, lifting it up to reveal her shoes.

"Well I never!" says Sergeant Norfolk. "White boots! Wherever did you get those, young lady?"

"She'll have made a deal wi' the devil, nae doubt. She should be set alight at the stake," Maggie declares.

"Do I get a chance to speak?" asks Martha.

"Ye should respect yer elders!" orders Maggie.

"Yes, yes, that's right," Sergeant Norfolk blusters, "Miss Osborne here has no reason to be telling tales."

Martha looks at Maggie and at Sergeant Norfolk and she sighs. The sergeant doesn't seem to be quite as cross about everything as Maggie is, but he is obviously happy to go along with whatever Maggie suggests.

Martha wonders if she should try to break away and run into Johnny's house. But Johnny's family has a new baby to enjoy. She doesn't want to disturb them after they already said goodbye. Reluctantly, she allows Sergeant Norfolk to take hold of her arm and direct her along the path.

They reach the church and Martha is led inside. Up until now, Martha had thought that Maggie Osborne was just an annoying and angry woman, someone who was strangely fixated on witchcraft. Now she begins to wonder if Maggie could become dangerous, especially if the sergeant listens to everything Maggie tells him. Martha's heart starts to beat fast, and she says a quick prayer as she is jostled past the wooden seats.

"Is Major Talbot here?" she asks, thinking that the major was much more sensible than this duo.

"No," says the sergeant, "Major Talbot has gone to inspect the soldiers at the castle on Arran."

"What about Mr Hamilton?" she asks.

The sergeant shrugs his shoulders. "Don't worry, you'll be given a fair trial." He turns to Maggie, "We'll lock her in the tower. She will be questioned for three days until she confesses," and the sergeant leads Martha up the steps while Maggie follows behind.

"If ye tell me how ye do yer magic, I'll see that ye're let oot," Maggie hisses in Martha's ear. "I'll visit ye later," she adds.

They stop at the second floor where all the armour is stored. "We'll put her in the dry closet," says the sergeant, "I've got a key for that door," and Martha is pushed into one of the small side chambers. The door clangs shut, and she hears the key turn in the lock.

Martha finds herself in a room the size of a large cupboard. It is dirty and it smells awful. She has been locked in the old toilet cubicle. "Thanks," she mutters, "remind me to pack some disinfectant next time I visit the 17th century!" But she is thankful to be rid of Maggie and Sergeant Norfolk, thankful to have been left alone. Now she just needs to escape to the 21st century one more time.

There is no chair in this room, but Martha doesn't care. She finds the cleanest looking bit of floor space in the corner nearest the door, sits down and rests her back and head against the wall. While she was being escorted up the stairs, Martha was thinking about how she has managed to return to her own time each day. She realises that she doesn't need a chair or a pew or a bash on the head. She simply needs to fall asleep in a safe place, and Martha is certain she is safe here in the old tower because she feels it has been watching over her all week. The bells in the tower called her to help Johnny's family, and now she has completed her mission.

She has had an overwhelming afternoon and is totally exhausted. Martha closes her eyes knowing that she will soon drift off and soon return to the present day. But just before she falls asleep, she chuckles as she thinks about the look that Maggie Osborne will have on her face when she opens the locked closet door and finds no-one inside!

XX

Present Day

Katie and Aunty Mary enter the dressing room on the 2nd Floor of the tower. They find Martha sleeping next to the box of hats in the little side chamber.

"Martha! Have you been here all the time? Did you sleep through the whole play?!" Katie asks.

"What?" says Martha, waking up with a yawn and sensing the much sweeter-smelling air. "Have I missed the play? Oh no! I'm sorry."

Aunty Mary has an astonished look on her face.

"Oh, Aunty Mary, I'm really sorry, have you been looking for me? I just needed a nap, I didn't mean to cause any worries."

"No, not at all love, actually I feel a bit bad," answers Martha's aunt. "I did struggle trying to see where you were when the procession first came out of the tower, but we were sat near the back, and all you girls looked the same with your bonnets on. Oh dear, your mum and I must have mistaken someone else for you, sorry, Martha. I got completely caught up in the play. It was only after it all finished, and Katie said she'd lost sight of you that we got a little bit concerned, but we found you quickly enough."

"Where is Mum?" asks Martha.

"She was coming up the stairs behind us, but she stopped to talk to someone," says Katie.

"I'm here!" their mum announces, poking her head around the corner. Martha jumps up and gives her mum a hug.

"Are you okay, Martha?" asks Mum.

"I'm fine. I've just been incredibly tired this week."

"Well, you'll be a teenager in a couple of years, and then we'll never get you out of your bed!"

"It's a pity you missed the play though," states Katie. "It was fun pretending to be in the 17th century."

"I don't mind," says Martha. "I'm really very happy to be right here in the 21st century. Is Dad here too? And where's Harry and Uncle Porridge?" she asks, keen to ensure that all her family are there with her in her real time.

"They've gone to play football on the Low Green, but they'll be back soon," answers Mum.

"Let's go home and have some dinner, and then we can light the fire in your room," adds Aunty Mary. "Did you get the marshmallows?"

"Yes, I did," says Martha, checking her pocket. "But ... mmh ... I don't have them anymore. You may find this hard to believe, but I gave them to someone who has never had marshmallows before, and who may never have them again."

"That sounds very intriguing," says Mum.

"It sounds to me like you ate the lot!" says Katie, "but I don't mind. I ate most of that tablet we bought, and I couldn't eat another sweet thing today if you paid me!"

* * * * * * *

As they walk back to their house Martha hears an ambulance siren in the distance, possibly dashing to the scene of an accident or taking a patient to hospital. Martha knows that Johnny would never have heard a noise like that. She looks around her. People are still in the grounds of the tower taking photos, and she notices the modern clothes they are wearing and the phones they are speaking into. She sees lamp posts and cars, TV aerials and satellite dishes on chimneys, drains in the gutters for sewage pipes and tarmac on the roads. She breathes in and the air smells clean and fresh. All of that is different from in Johnny's time.

But the ground she is walking over is the same ground where people walked to the church to worship God for hundreds of years. It is the same ground where soldiers once marched and built a huge citadel. It is the same ground where ordinary people worked as best as they could to help their families thrive despite sickness and hardships. Martha knows that Johnny and his family loved and cared about each other just as much as she and her family do. That hasn't changed at all.

She looks up at the old church tower standing there straight and strong, watching them all walk over the same ground where people have lived and loved for hundreds of years. She hopes it will be there for centuries to come.

Martha

Sunday

XXI

Present Day

Martha wakes to the sound of Katie and Harry fighting over the lap-top. She pulls the pillow over her head, trying to block out their voices, so that she can have a few more minutes of sleep.

"Please Katie! You've been on it for ages, it's my turn," begs Harry.

"I'm sorry, but it's nobody's turn on the lap-top. It's time for you all to be getting up and dressed," says Mum as she enters the room. "Remember we've got church this morning and a lot of packing to do."

Martha immediately thinks of the big, old church, but she heard no bells chiming this morning. The tower didn't call her today, and she understands that her job in the 17th century is over. She briefly wonders if Johnny caught any rabbits this morning and then straight away realises that it's a daft thought. It's hundreds of years since Johnny caught any rabbits.

"How are you feeling sleepy-head?" Mum has walked over to Martha's bed and she pushes the pillow aside and strokes Martha's head. Martha yawns and stretches, "I'm fine Mum. I think I needed that sleep, it's the first morning I haven't woken up early all week."

"Okay, time to get up now though," says Mum, and she notices Martha's school book, '17th Century Britain,' on the floor by the bed. "Did you manage to do your homework?" she asks, "the history essay?"

"I haven't finished it yet, but it's going to be easy. It will be all about 17th century life in Ayr. In fact I can't wait to write it."

"Well that's good news. You've never been keen on history before."

"I love history now!" proclaims Martha, "and Mum, I was thinking last night that I may want to be a midwife when I grow up. What do I need to study for that?"

"Well I'm not sure," says Mum, "that's certainly something to think about. You should probably ask the school careers adviser. But for now, please, let's get a move on. Check under the beds and in the rooms downstairs so we don't leave anything behind."

Martha is left wondering about the conversation she will have with her careers adviser. What should she say if she's asked why she wants to be a midwife?! She can't wait to tell her friend Sarah though!

* * * * * * *

When she enters the kitchen for breakfast, Martha is glad to find that only her Uncle Peter is there. She believes there must be a connection between Johnny's family and her uncle. She knows that they have the same surname, but lots of people have the same surname. She hopes to find more proof.

"Uncle Porridge," she asks, "have your family always lived in Ayr?"

"No, but my parents used to come here every year to visit a great uncle of my father's. At some point they decided to stay, and I was born here. I moved away for a while, but I soon came back. I belong in Ayr."

This helps Martha a bit, but it doesn't prove anything, so she probes some more. "That great uncle that your parents used to visit, do you know, was he your father's only uncle? I know you don't have many relatives."

"Not many relatives! Are you kidding?! I have a huge family. I've got heaps of aunties, uncles, cousins and ..."

"But the other day," Martha butts in, "when you were working on your car in the garage, I'm sure you said ..."

A shiver runs down Martha's back. So something has changed. It isn't like she has drastically changed the course of history by introducing a computer to the 17th century, but things have changed. She helped a mum and a baby to live, that might not have survived, and in doing so a whole big family has flourished.

Uncle Porridge is looking at her, waiting for her to finish her sentence. "Oh, I'm sorry, I must have picked it up wrong," she says, "but I do have another question for you."

"Fire away."

"Do you have any idea why your mum and dad called you Peter?" she ventures.

"Well, there have always been lots of Peter's in the family, so it was probably just a name that came readily to mind. Actually my mum wanted to call me Iain, but the midwife told her she shouldn't do that. She said Iain is the same name as John in Gaelic and my elder brother was already called John."

Martha's face lights up. "Really?! Your mum was going to call you Iain, and you have a brother called John?" and she chuckles, remembering a similar conversation between Johnny's mother and Mrs Craig over what to call the new baby.

"Aye, he lives abroad, but he's always been known as Johnny, never John. Mum said she wanted to give him a name that wouldn't be shortened, but of course it got lengthened instead."

Martha continues to chuckle, shaking her head in disbelief.

"But what's so funny?" asks her uncle.

"It's not exactly funny," says Martha, "it's kind of freaky really! I've heard that story before." And she smiles broadly as she thinks back to her very first chat with Johnny."

Uncle Porridge is somewhat puzzled. He doesn't remember ever telling that story before, but he is glad that he made his niece smile. "Now Martha. Are you ready for some breakfast? What would you like to eat?"

"Porridge of course! Please, Uncle Porridge, make me some porridge!"

****

The car is all packed up. They have a final look around to make sure they haven't left anything, and then it's time for hugs and kisses as they say their farewells. The car pulls away and Aunty Mary and Uncle Porridge wave goodbye from the door-step. The children wave back shouting, "Bye! Bye!" until their aunt and uncle are out of sight, hidden by the trees in front of their house.

Martha keeps waving the longest. "Goodbye Tower! Goodbye Johnny!" she calls out of the car window. And she keeps waving until all she can see of St. John's Tower is its flag fluttering in the breeze, a blue flag with a diagonal white cross.

"Did you all have a good time?" asks Dad.

"It was great," says Harry.

"Yes, it was fab," agrees Katie.

"Aye," adds Martha, "it was braw!"

"Braw?" questions Dad.

"Brilliant."

"Well, we've got a long drive ahead. I'd love to hear all about it. Especially if you're going to tell me who that Johnny is you were shouting goodbye to Martha!"

"I will," says Martha, "in fact I have quite a story to tell you." Katie and Harry simultaneously turn their heads fixedly towards Martha. "Just wait," she tells them.

They are routeing through the busy part of town, and Martha can see that her dad is concentrating on the traffic. She wants everyone to be giving her their full attention before she starts her story. She keeps them waiting until they reach the main road.

"Are you all sitting comfortably?" she asks, "then I'll begin. This is the tale of a Scottish tower ..."

St. John's Tower, Ayr

Two short films showing the interior of the tower can be found at:

http://www.stjohnstower.btck.co.uk/

The story is over, but if you want to impress people with your knowledge, you can read these historical notes too!

The Church of St. John the Baptist, Ayr

St. John's Tower is all that remains•of Ayr's original parish church, which was dedicated to St. John the Baptist, the patron saint of Ayr. The large, cross-shaped church was built in the late 12th century; however there may have been a more basic church on the same site for hundreds of years before that; St. Ninian having introduced Christianity to southern Scotland in 397AD.

St. John's is thought to have been one of the most splendid churches in Scotland, with a great gothic window and at least eight altars in addition to the high altar. The bell tower was a later addition to the original church, added in the 14th or 15th century.

Notable visitors include: Robert the Bruce, who held Parliament there in April 1315 after Bannockburn; James IV, who made numerous offerings for masses to be said in St. John's; and possibly Mary Queen of Scots, who is said to have 'supped and slept at St. John of Ayr,' although this may refer to the town, rather than the church. St. John's was Roman Catholic until the middle of the 16th century.

In 1560, St. John's became a Reformed Church under an Act of Parliament. John Knox led the protestant reformation in Scotland and he is known to have preached in Ayr. He had strong links to Ayrshire, and his second wife came from Ochiltree.

In the 1650s, Oliver Cromwell's troops established a fort and citadel in Ayr and took over the church for a chapel, storehouse, armoury and watch-tower. In 1654 Cromwell helped to fund the building of a new church, also called St.

John the Baptist, now more commonly known as Ayr's Auld Kirk.

Following Cromwell's death in 1658 and the restoration of King Charles II in 1660, the demilitarised fort, including the former church of St. John, was gifted by the crown to the 7th Earl of Eglinton as compensation for the losses suffered by his family while supporting the royalist cause. The fort grounds became the barony of Montgomerieston, a private estate. The original St. John's Church was last used as a place of worship in 1687.

The Tower

By 1726, the body of the church was demolished. Some of its stones were used to build a steeple for the tolbooth in the Sandgate. The tower was left standing as it was an important navigational aid, guiding mariners to the harbour entrance. The bells were probably removed from the tower at that time.

In 1852 gunsmith John Miller returned to Ayrshire from India where he had made his fortune. He purchased the barony of Montgomerieston and locally became known as 'Baron Miller' as he set about transforming the old church tower into a suitably baronial-looking residence. John Murdoch added extensions to it in Gothic style and Miller disposed of most of the rest of the fort estate as house plots, keeping a walled area around his home for himself.

Following John Miller's death in 1910, the tower was acquired by the 4th Marquess of Bute. He had inherited the enthusiasm of his father, the 3rd Marquess, for using the family fortune to preserve and restore historic buildings. He engaged architect James Kennedy Hunter to return the old tower to its appearance as sketched by John Slezer in the seventeenth century. Miller's additions were removed in 1913-14 and extensive restoration work resulted in St John's Tower as it stands today. The 5th Marquess of Bute gifted it to the town of Ayr in 1949.

The interior of the tower can be viewed on Doors Open Day (usually in September each year) when access is facilitated by members of the Friends of St. John's Tower (FrOST). Visits may also be organised by arrangement with South Ayrshire Council.

Ayr's Oldest School

Ayr's earliest school is first mentioned in records as being at the Church of St. John the Baptist in 1233. It was possibly sited in an outbuilding of the church. The original teachers were church chaplains, teaching Latin and music. English (reading and writing) was added to the curriculum in 1559 when the church school became a burgh school. From 1600, schooling was also offered to girls.

The school moved out of the church in 1602 and took up residence in a two-roomed cottage overlooking the harbour; where it expanded and became Ayr Academy.

In the 1650s, church services were held in the school for three years during the army's occupation of the church. In the 17th century, the school masters, now appointed by the town council, were expected to take on additional duties connected to the church (the church chaplains having been dismissed post-reformation). The school masters received additional income for assisting the church minister in various duties and acting as the Session Clerk, keeping business records.

John Hamilton was 'Master of the Schule of Air' from 1643 to 1649.

Colonel Matthew Alured's Commonwealth Regiment of Foot

In 1650, during the third English civil war, Oliver Cromwell's parliamentarian forces invaded Scotland, taking control of the south of the country. Colonel Matthew Alured took command of the Commonwealth Regiment of Foot in August 1650. The regiment originated from Yorkshire, but was sent to Scotland, and in 1651 the soldiers took part in the siege of Tantallon Castle, North Berwick. In March 1652 they were ordered to Ayr.

Colonel Alured was the first commander of the fort in Ayr, and Cromwell's Citadel was largely completed during his time there. Detachments from the regiment served in a number of small garrisons in the Highlands and Islands, including Arran.

By autumn 1654, the regiment had been posted away, replaced by a regiment under the command of Colonel Thomas Cooper. Alured's regiment served in Scotland throughout the 1650s; however, Alured was relieved of command after openly opposing Cromwell. Thomas Talbot was promoted to succeed Alured in June 1655.

The regiment was disbanded at Tower Hill in London on Monday 19th November 1660. The Mercurius Publicus newspaper reported: "The soldiery appeared all very cheerful in laying down their arms, as they had formerly done in taking them up ... They gave many volleys of shot, and made several other expressions of their willingness to part with those arms which they desired to keep no longer than till his Majesty was restored to his Kingdome."

17th Century Witchcraft

To be accused of witchcraft in the 16th and 17th centuries was a very serious matter. Thousands were prosecuted throughout Europe and America, and witchcraft was a capital offence. Public execution by burning was the usual outcome for those found guilty, regardless of the haphazard way that trials were often carried out. It is thought that some of the accused were worshipping the devil; however, many innocents were convicted of being possessed by the devil when it is likely they suffered from mental health disorders. Others were caught up in the witch hunts because of their interest in medicinal practices. All were treated quite barbarically by today's standards.

There are records in Ayr of several women who suffered as a result of being condemned witches (including Janet Smyllie, who died in 1649 after being confined to the tolbooth on suspicion of witchcraft). There are no official records relating to Maggie Osborne's trial and prosecution for witchcraft, yet she is widely thought to have been Ayr's last witch. Many legends exist about her exploits.

The Scots language words used in this book are from:
The dialect of Robert Burns as spoken in Central Ayrshire, (Sir James Wilson, Oxford University Press, 1923)

aboot	*about*	bairn	*child*
anither	*another*	bide	*stay, wait*
aw	*all*	bonnie	*beautiful*
aye	*yes*	braw	*excellent*